Joanna was hurt by Matt's insinuations

"What's the matter?" he demanded. "After the way you behaved the other evening, what am I supposed to think?"

"That was different," she exclaimed. "That was you! For heaven's sake, Matt, what do you think I am?"

"I don't know," he muttered. "How do I know your reactions to men you meet?"

"Well, I don't go to bed with them," she retaliated. "Just because of daddy's death you see yourself as some sort of father figure."

Matthew forced her to face him. "Right now I surely don't feel like your father! Joanna," he said hoarsely, "we have to talk...."

"What's there to say?" she breathed. "Oh, Matt, you want to touch me, I know you do." Her hands reached for him, and parting her lips, she pressed herself against him.

ANNE MATHER
is also the author of these

Harlequin Presents

322—THE JUDAS TRAP
329—LURE OF EAGLES
335—APOLLO'S SEED
347—HELL OR HIGH WATER
351—SPIRIT OF ATLANTIS
376—WHISPER OF DARKNESS
382—SANDSTORM
402—IMAGES OF LOVE
405—EDGE OF TEMPTATION
429—A HAUNTING COMPULSION
436—FORBIDDEN FLAME
449—CASTLES OF SAND
468—INNOCENT OBSESSION
490—DUELLING FIRE
509—SMOKESCREEN
530—IMPETUOUS MASQUERADE
546—SEASON OF MISTS
563—A PASSIONATE AFFAIR
586—AN ELUSIVE DESIRE

and these

Harlequin Romances

1487—CHARLOTTE'S HURRICANE
1574—LORD OF ZARACUS
1600—THE RELUCTANT GOVERNESS
1631—MASQUERADE
1656—AUTUMN OF THE WITCH

Many of these titles are available at your local bookseller.

For a free catalog listing all available Harlequin Romances
and Harlequin Presents, send your name and address to:

HARLEQUIN READER SERVICE
1440 South Priest Drive, Tempe, AZ 85281
Canadian address: Stratford, Ontario N5A 6W2

ANNE MATHER

cage of shadows

Harlequin Books

TORONTO • NEW YORK • LOS ANGELES • LONDON
AMSTERDAM • PARIS • SYDNEY • HAMBURG
STOCKHOLM • ATHENS • TOKYO • MILAN

Harlequin Presents first edition July 1983
ISBN 0-373-10610-6

Original hardcover edition published in 1983
by Mills & Boon Limited

CHAPTER ONE

'Do it,' said Evan urgently. 'What have you got to lose? And more importantly, think what you've got to gain.'

'Yes.'

Joanna pushed her large-framed spectacles up her nose and cupped her chin with one hand. A tall girl, with a curtain of silky dark brown hair that fell about her shoulders, she looked rather pensive at present, the long green eyes, which she privately considered her best feature, opaque now behind their shield of tinted glass.

'How else are you ever going to afford to go to art college?' Evan persisted. 'You told me yourself that Marcia was unlikely to help you.'

'I know.'

Joanna sighed. It certainly was a temptation. With the kind of money Evan Price was offering, she might even be able to afford her own flat, and to be independent of her stepmother would be worth so much more. Judging by the rumblings recently, Marcia expected her to get out and find herself a job, and just because her father had expected her to go to art school there was no reason to think his widow would sponsor her. On the contrary, Marcia had made it clear, right from the beginning, when Joanna's father died so suddenly without leaving any provision for his daughter, that she did not consider herself bound to support her.

'Consider it a holiday,' Evan was saying

persuasively. 'A month in Florida, in the middle of an English winter! What could be better? Have you any idea how much people pay to enjoy the kind of break I'm offering you for free?'

'I'm sure it's a marvellous opportunity,' Joanna conceded doubtfully, and the florid-faced man sitting across from her raised his eyes to the ceiling.

'Joanna, believe me, if it was anyone else but you, I wouldn't be offering this kind of money. But—well, your father was a friend of mine, and I feel I owe something to his memory——'

'And the fact that I happened to have a passing acquaintance with Matthew Wilder has nothing to do with it?' put in Joanna, with unexpected cynicism. 'Evan, I know what you're offering, and I know why. I just don't know if I want to do it, that's all.'

'Why not?'

'Because—because he obviously wants to avoid the media. Why else would he choose to go and live out in Florida? His work has always been in Europe and Africa.'

'Who knows why he's gone out there? Maybe he's discovered some new drug and he's trying it out. That's what I want you to find out. Joanna, Matthew Wilder is still big news. And he's been out of the public eye for almost three years! Now we know where he is, at least let's give it a try.'

Joanna pursed her lips. 'Marcia had no right to give you Daddy's diaries. They were personal.'

'They're also worth a lot of bread,' declared Evan flatly. 'And Marcia was never one to shy at the main chance. Besides,' he tried to reassure her, 'your father was one of this century's foremost writers. It was a tragedy he was killed like that, but his diaries belong to his readers. Your father himself would agree with me.'

Joanna bent her head. 'The private addresses should have been torn out. My father wouldn't approve of you betraying his confidence.'

'What the hell!' exploded Evan noisily. 'Drew's been dead all of five months, Joanna. What he would or would not have done isn't relevant. For three years, Wilder's lived the life of a recluse. No one knew where he was. Now *we* have his address—rightly or wrongly. Would you rather I sent a news team out there? Spread the word around Fleet Street, and have every two-bit reporter with a telephoto lens crawling over the island?'

'No.' Joanna was sure about that. 'But what makes you think Uncle Matt will see me? I was eight years old when I last saw him. Eleven years ago! I doubt he'll even remember me.'

'You're Andrew Holland's daughter. He'll remember you.'

Joanna shook her head. 'I don't know.'

'Well, make up your mind. I need a decision. I've no intention of sitting on this for too long.'

Joanna hesitated. 'But why is it so urgent? You said yourself, it's five months since—since my father was killed.'

'Marcia only handed the diaries over two weeks ago,' admitted Evan shortly. 'I don't think she realised they were of any value until your father's solicitor suggested the idea.'

'Howard Rogers?' Joanna's lips curled. 'Oh, yes, it would be Howard who suggested it. My father's privacy would mean nothing to him.'

Evan frowned. 'Do I detect a note of bitterness?'

'No.' Joanna was indignant, and then she

sighed. 'Well, not really. It's just that Howard's
been around a lot more since Daddy died. I
sometimes wonder exactly what his intentions are.'

'Yes.' Evan was thoughtful now. 'Well, it has to
be said, he hasn't had much success on your
behalf, has he? I should have thought that as your
father's solicitor, he would have suggested it was
Marcia's duty to provide you with an allowance,
at least.'

Joanna made no comment. She was reluctant to
criticise her stepmother's motives, even to Evan,
who had been her father's publisher for the past
fifteen years. But it was hard to justify the mean
streak in Marcia, that caused her to ignore her
stepdaughter's feelings, and create the kind of
situation where Joanna felt obligated to support
herself. It should not have been necessary; her
father had died a wealthy man. But such were his
feelings for the woman he had married ten years
after his wife's death, he had been blind to the
flaws in her character. Joanna had no doubt he
had believed Marcia would take care of his
daughter should anything happen to him. But she
couldn't help wishing he had not been so
unworldly, and left her at least enough to live on.

'Five thousand pounds, Joanna.' Evan interrupted her train of thought. 'Five thousand
pounds and expenses. I can't say fairer than that,
can I?'

Joanna avoided his gaze, glancing round the
restaurant where he had brought her for lunch
with troubled eyes. It was rather an exclusive
restaurant, and on any other occasion she would
have appreciated his generosity. But no matter
how she tried, she couldn't rid herself of the notion
that this was all a deliberate ploy to get her into a

frame of mind where she would jump at his proposition, equating the kind of money he was offering with the lifestyle she had grown up to expect.

'Five thousand pounds,' she murmured half inaudibly, but he heard her.

'All right, six, then,' he declared, 'but it's my last word,' and Joanna felt even worse that he should think she was trying to bargain.

'I—can I think about it?' she asked at last, lifting her bespectacled eyes to his. 'I mean—you do appreciate, I—I have commitments.'

'What commitments?'

Evan was sceptical, and Joanna assumed an aloof expression. 'I do have friends, you know,' she replied, stung by his indifference, and stifling his impatience, Evan acquiesced.

'Okay,' he said shortly. 'I'll give you—forty-eight hours to think it over. If you haven't contacted me in that time, I'll consider the offer rejected, right?'

'Right.' Joanna spoke less confidently now. It was all very well making proud statements about commitments, but the truth was, if she didn't take this chance, she would have to take a job—any job—to supplement her dwindling resources.

'Right.' Evan lifted a hand and summoned the waiter. 'You know my number. I'll be waiting for your call. Just don't make me wait too long.'

Going home on the bus, Joanna wondered what he would have said if she had challenged his bland bravado. After all, if Matthew Wilder had intentionally cut himself off from his friends and colleagues, what chance might a stranger have of making contact with him? Evan knew this, or he would never have contacted her. He knew that a news team from one of the specialist magazines he published might never stand a chance of seeing Wilder, let alone talking with him, and if she, Joanna, refused to co-operate, he could easily have to abandon the whole idea.

From Matthew Wilder's point of view, that could only be for the best, she reflected ruefully. The man obviously wanted to remain undisturbed. Was it fair for her, no matter what her connections, to consider invading his privacy? Of course it wasn't. It was reprehensible, and she knew it. Particularly as Evan's suggestion had been that she should pretend she was holidaying in the area, and had come upon his house unaware.

Joanna closed her eyes in disgust. It was all so corny! Who would believe it? Least of all a man like Matthew Wilder, who had years of experience in dealing with the media.

Fifteen years ago, when his first book was accepted for publication, Andrew Holland had bought a tall Victorian house, in an unfashionable suburb in north London. Since then, the suburb had become fashionable, and now the house was worth quite a lot of money, but her father had never wanted to move. Joanna couldn't really remember living anywhere else, but now, as she walked along Ashworth Terrace, she couldn't help wondering how long it would be before Marcia decided to realise this investment too.

There was a car parked at the kerb in front of the house, and Joanna recognised it with a deepening sense of depression. It was Howard Rogers' car, and the fact that the solicitor was here meant that she and Marcia would have no chance to talk privately. She had decided on the bus to talk to her stepmother, ask her what she thought she should do; but now that Howard was here, any private discussions would have to wait.

Joanna let herself into the house with her key, pausing in the carpeted hall to remove her fur-lined suede jacket. It was a chilly afternoon, and although she had scarcely noticed the temperature as she walked the couple of hundred yards from the bus stop, now that she was indoors, she lifted her shoulders appreciatively in the warmth from the heating system.

She could hear no sound of voices from the library where Marcia generally entertained visitors, and she was about to mount the stairs to her room when the housekeeper, Mrs Morris, appeared from the kitchen.

'They're in the library,' she confided in an undertone, surprising the girl. 'Or at least they were half an hour ago. I was just going to bring some tea. I'll put an extra cup on the tray.'

Joanna bit her lip. Mrs Morris's affection had sustained her during the long months since her father's death, but even to please her, she couldn't intrude on her stepmother's privacy without an invitation.

'It's all right, Mrs Morris,' she said. 'I'd really rather go up and change. I'll come down and have a cup of tea with you in the kitchen afterwards, if you don't mind.'

'Bless you, you know you're——' began the housekeeper, only to break off abruptly as the door to the right of the hall opened and a burly man of medium height appeared in the aperture. Wearing a city suit, Howard Rogers, as always, was dressed to fit his role as her father's—and now her stepmother's—legal adviser, but Joanna uneasily retained the notion that his appearance belied the true measure of his character. She didn't like him. She never had. And she drew back now, wishing he had not overheard their low-voiced conversation.

'Joanna!' he exclaimed heartily. 'I thought it must be you. Marcia said you'd be out for the rest of the afternoon, but obviously she was wrong. Come in, come in. I'd like to have a word with you.'

Giving Mrs Morris a rueful look, Joanna acknowledged his greeting and stepped past him into the library. The last thing she needed right now was to play gooseberry with him and her stepmother. Marcia would not appreciate it, and most definitely, nor would she.

But to her surprise, the library was unoccupied, and when Howard closed the door behind them she glanced round almost apprehensively. She had never been alone with him before, and although she knew he was old enough to be her father, she felt an unwelcome sense of anxiety at the sudden glitter in his pale eyes.

'I—where's Marcia?' she asked, trying not to sound as nervous as she felt, and Howard walked across the room to take up his stance before the fireplace. Although the house was centrally heated, her father had always kept an open fire in the library, and the solicitor put his hands behind his back to warm them at the blaze.

'Marcia is getting changed,' he replied, after positioning himself to his satisfaction. 'I'm taking her out to dinner this evening. I thought we'd drive into the country. I know a rather attractive hotel in Sussex, with an extremely good wine cellar.' He paused, rocking backwards and forwards on his heels and toes. 'Wine is so important to a meal, don't you think so, Joanna? Food is a necessity, but wine adds that something extra, the gilding on the gingerbread, so to speak.'

'Er—what did you want to talk to me about, Mr Rogers?' enquired Joanna, blinking rather owlishly behind her tortoiseshell rims. She had no wish to prolong this conversation, and she didn't like the way Howard was acting. As if this was his home, and she was the visitor.

'There's no hurry,' averred Howard smoothly. 'Marcia will be ages yet—you know what she's like. It will take her half an hour to decide what dress she's going to wear.'

Joanna expelled her breath resignedly. 'Mr Rogers——'

'Howard. Why don't you call me Howard?' he suggested jovially. 'After all, we're friends, aren't we? And you're not a little girl any more, Joanna. By no means, no. You're quite a young lady. How old are you now? Seventeen? Eighteen?'

'I'm nineteen, and I think you know that, Mr Rogers,' responded Joanna tautly. 'Please, get to the point. I—er—I'm going out this evening myself.'

'Are you?' Howard's reddish-grey brows arched. 'Where are you going?'

'I don't think that's any of your business,' retorted Joanna with some heat. 'Mr Rogers——'

'Oh, very well.' His thin mouth tightened. 'If you will persist in this childishness, I have no option but to treat you as one. Marcia—Marcia and I—your stepmother and I, that is——' Joanna's nerves jangled, '—Marcia and I are going to get married.'

'To get married!'

If there had been a chair behind her, Joanna would have sank into it, but there wasn't, and she stood there on legs that threatened any moment to give out on her, staring at him as if he had pointed a gun at her head.

'Don't look so horrified.' Howard shifted a little uncomfortably nevertheless. 'It shouldn't come as such a shock to you. You must have realised that Marcia and I were—well, close friends at least?'

Joanna shook her head. She couldn't speak. She felt as if her throat had closed up, and she stood there like an automaton, frozen in an attitude of dumb disbelief.

'For goodness' sake!' Howard's initial sense of discomfort gave way to a cajoling impatience. 'Don't look like that, Joanna, or I shall begin to think you don't like me, and I know that's not true.' He stepped diffidently across the floor towards her, halting in front of her and looking encouragingly into her pale stunned features. Because he was not a tall man, they were almost on eye-level terms, and she longed to shrink away from that fawning insincerity. 'Joanna,' he said, wheedlingly, 'this isn't like you. This isn't like my pretty little girl.' He lifted his hand and brushed a strand of dark hair back from her forehead. 'Such a lovely girl,' he breathed, his voice thickening. 'If your father had just been a little less besotted——'

'Don't touch me!' With an abrupt movement, Joanna recoiled from the pudgy hand that lightly grazed her cheek, and Howard's expression hardened as she shuddered in distaste.

'There's no need for that, Joanna,' he declared harshly. 'I should watch my step if I were you. It's only through my good offices that you're still here, in this house. Marcia would have cast you out long ago. Only I persuaded her that you weren't ready, that you needed time——'

'—that it wouldn't look good for my father's widow to throw out his only daughter within weeks of his funeral!' snapped Joanna in disgust. 'Don't pretend you had any real thought for my feelings.'

'You're wrong, Joanna.' Howard clenched his fists angrily. 'If it hadn't been for me, you'd have been working in some shop or café by now, slogging your guts out all day, and dragging yourself home to some sleazy bedsitter! As it is——'

'As it is, I'm to be thrown out now, is that it?'

'No.' Howard took another step towards her. 'Not if you play your cards right.'

'Not if I play my cards right?' Joanna stood her ground, staring at him distrustfully. 'What is that supposed to mean? What are you talking about?'

'I'm talking about art school, that's what I'm talking about,' exclaimed Howard triumphantly. 'That is what you want to do, isn't it? Go to art school?'

'Well—yes——'

'Very well, then,' Howard hesitated a moment, before putting his hot fingers beneath her chin and tilting her face to his. 'If you stop treating me like a leper, I'll promise to put in a good word for you. Between us, we should be able to persuade Marcia——'

Joanna was appalled, but she forced herself to remain motionless as his thumb rubbed insinuatingly along her jawline. Dear Heaven, her thoughts raced, what was he suggesting? That she should allow him to—to—— Her mind baulked at the obvious conclusion, but her spirits rose again at the thought of what Marcia would say when she told her the truth——

'I mean,' Howard was going on, his whisky-scented breath fanning her cheek, 'you know that if your father had made you his heir——'

The sound of the handle of the door being turned effected the reaction Joanna was about to make. It caused Howard to step abruptly away from her, and by the time Marcia Holland came into the room, he was back in his position before the fire, apparently conducting a casual exchange with her stepdaughter.

Marcia Holland was small and blonde and petite, the exact antithesis of Joanna. Having seen pictures of her own mother, Joanna had sometimes wondered whether Andrew Holland had married Marcia because she was the absolute opposite of what his first wife had been. Joanna's mother had been an extremely capable woman. Marcia appeared not. She behaved the way men expected a woman like her to behave. Because she looked so small and frail, she adopted an air of ingenuous fragility, and she always succeeded in getting her own way, because she looked so helpless. Only Joanna knew she wasn't helpless; anything but. Marcia's outward appearance was only a façade; underneath she was a very determined woman.

Now, she closed the door and advanced into the room, her gaze flickering briefly over her stepdaughter before moving on to the man by the fire. Holding out her hands towards Howard, she moved into the circle of his arm, and then turned to face Joanna, as if anxious for her approval.

'Has Howard told you our news?' she asked, in the little-girl voice she effected whenever any man was within earshot, and Joanna, endeavouring to recover from the two shocks she had received, took a deep breath.

'He—he's told me you plan to get married,' she replied rather huskily. 'I—I was surprised. I had no idea you had that in mind.'

Marcia's brittle blue eyes hardened. 'I don't have to discuss my affairs with you, Joanna,' she said, the baby-soft voice belying the pointedness of the words. She glanced up at the man beside her, her diminutive size complementing his height. 'It happened so quickly, didn't it, darling? We didn't have time to discuss it with anyone.'

'You're so right,' applauded Howard warmly, and the duplicity of his behaviour made Joanna feel physically sick. 'But Joanna knows all about it now. I've put her in the picture, so to speak.' His eyes flicked insolently in the girl's direction. 'Isn't that right, Joanna?'

Joanna's lips felt stiff, but she knew she had to speak. She would not—she could not—let him get away with it. 'I don't know that Marcia would agree with you,' she retorted contemptuously. 'I'm sure she's totally in the dark about what you have in mind.'

Marcia's blue eyes darted swiftly up at the man within whose arm she was nestling. 'Howard?' she murmured questioningly. 'What is she talking about? What do you have in mind?'

Later, Joanna realised she had played right into Howard's hands by accusing him outright. But just then she could only stare at him in outrage as he expertly negotiated this unexpected attack. Instead of rushing to his own defence as Joanna had anticipated, he took a leaf out of Marcia's book and assumed a rueful expression, answering her reluctantly, as if betraying a confidence.

'I'm afraid—well, Joanna doesn't entirely approve of the place I'm taking you for our honeymoon,' he conceded with a convincing sigh. 'I suppose—the villa was her father's, and——'

'The villa!' exclaimed Joanna, doing the unforgivable and losing her temper. 'The villa wasn't even mentioned! He made a pass at me, Marcia! He told me that if I'd been Daddy's heir instead of you——'

'That's enough!' With a muffled ejaculation Marcia pulled herself away from the solicitor and regarded her stepdaughter with cold loathing. 'That will do, Joanna. I will not listen to any more. How dare you? How dare you stand there and vilify the man I intend to marry?'

'It's the truth,' protested Joanna wearily. 'For Heaven's sake, Marcia, it's not you he's interested in, it's Daddy's money! He virtually told me——'

'Be quiet!' Marcia's hand stung across Joanna's hot cheek, successfully silencing her stepdaughter. 'I think you'd better leave,' she went on icily. 'I've known for some time that you hated me, Joanna, that you were jealous of me. But I never thought you'd stoop to telling lies to get even with me——'

'I'm not lying.' Joanna looked at Howard, as if hoping to find some betraying emotion she could reveal to her stepmother, but his face was calm, sympathetic even. He looked as if he could think of no reason for this unwarranted attack, and only his eyes showed any real evidence of his feelings. 'Marcia, please——'

'I want you to leave us,' repeated her stepmother coldly. 'I will not put up with your selfishness a moment longer. Get out! And I don't just mean out of the library. I mean out of this house!'

CHAPTER TWO

JOANNA drove south through miles of open swampland, alert to the danger that some unwary alligator might step into the road in front of her. The man at the car-rental agency in Miami Beach had warned her that alligators were now protected by law, but Joanna suspected his aim was to inspire interest rather than warn of any serious hazard. She rather hoped she would meet an alligator, so long as she was safely inside the car, of course, but all she had seen so far were herons and wild geese, and, once, the long-necked beauty of a stork in flight.

She had spent the last couple of days in Miami Beach recovering from her jet-lag and endeavouring to get her bearings. She bought some maps and spent some time plotting her route to the Keys, but the temptation was to linger, and she was loath to leave the security of the hotel. Her room overlooked the salt-water creek at the front of the hotel, and beyond, the colour-washed villas of some of Miami Beach's wealthier inhabitants made an ideal backdrop to the luxury yachts that moored at the hotel overnight. At the back of the hotel, a soft sandy beach stretched to the ocean, and Joanna had swum in its translucent green waters, feeling the warmth and relaxation of the sun unloosening the nerves that were wound tight within her.

She didn't want to think about England. She didn't want to remember that awful scene she had

had with Marcia, or recollect that when she returned to London she would have to find somewhere to live. Mrs Morris had been marvellous, of course, but she couldn't continue to depend on her help. Nevertheless, she had been grateful when the housekeeper had found her temporary accommodation with her sister and her husband in Fulham, and for the present that was where all her personal belongings were stored.

Evan had been delighted when she had rung him and confirmed that she would accept his offer. She didn't bore him with her reasons for accepting. She simply let him think she was doing it for the money, which she supposed, if she was honest with herself, she was. But there was more, so much more, to this escape from England. It seemed as if, since her father died, she had been living in limbo, and only now was she beginning to take a hold of her life. For so long she had let things slide, waiting for Marcia to make a move. Well, she had made the move instead, albeit impulsively, and it was up to her now to make a success of her future. She tried not to feel bitter; bitterness was a negative emotion. But even so, it was painful to think of Howard Rogers living in her father's house, using her father's things, sleeping in her father's bed . . .

Thirty miles south of Homestead, the swamps gave way to the blue waters of Florida Bay, and the highway swept over its first bridge on to the island of Key Largo. Although Joanna was intrigued by the signs indicating the John Pennekamp Coral Reef State Park, she pressed on, following the highway as it leapfrogged its way over a series of long bridges to other islands with names like Islamorada and Long Key and Bahia Honda.

The cooler morning when she had set off gave way to the heat of noon, and Joanna was glad that the car had air-conditioning. Just now, she would have been sweating, even in the cotton vest and shorts which were her only attire, and although there was usually a breeze to offset the higher temperatures, sitting on a sticky car seat was not the most comfortable way to travel.

It was after one o'clock when she reached Mango Key. The main highway intersected the island at the newer commercial quarter, but having read her guide books well, Joanna took the road that led to the older part of town. Her route took her along streets with a distinctly Spanish air, grilled balconies overhung with vines and bougainvillea, and pastel-tinted walls guarding inner courtyards where fountains played. At this time of the afternoon the streets were quiet, only an occasional horse-drawn vehicle meandering its way between rose-covered pergolas, carrying energetic tourists on a journey round the island. Joanna was able to stop and read the road signs without being harassed by other irate motorists, and she found the Hotel Conchas without too much difficulty.

She parked the car on the forecourt, and leaving her luggage in the trunk, walked the few yards between the parking area and the cool, air-conditioned freshness of the hotel. But even in those few yards she could feel the heat of the sun on her bare shoulders, and was glad her hair was thick enough to protect her head. She was glad, too, she had caught it up in a knot on top of her head. Already the back of her neck felt sticky, and its weight about her shoulders would have been unbearable.

The receptionist was Cuban, a dark-eyed, dark-skinned young man who eyed Joanna's long slim bare legs with appreciation as she crossed the marble-tiled foyer. Not for the first time since coming to Florida, she was made aware of her own femininity, and she adjusted her spectacles firmly, as if disclaiming any desire to draw attention to herself.

'I—good afternoon,' she murmured in a low voice, and then, clearing her throat, went on: 'My name's Holland, Joanna Holland. I phoned you from the hotel in Miami.'

'Ah yes, Miss Holland.' The young man's eyes assessed her as he consulted his ledger. 'You are a visitor from England, am I right? You are booked with us for two weeks.'

'Provisionally, yes,' agreed Joanna, moistening her upper lip and concentrating her attention on the entry in the book open on the desk. 'But I may stay longer. Will that be all right? I mean, you're not likely to get booked up or anything?'

'We can always hope,' remarked the young man humorously. 'But take it easy. I'm sure we can always accommodate you, Miss Holland.'

Joanna sighed. 'Er—my suitcases are out in my car. I just parked on the forecourt. Could someone . . .?'

A bell-boy was summoned and while Joanna filled in the necessary registration form, her luggage was brought in from the car and placed on a trolley, ready for direction.

'Room 447,' the receptionist advised at last, handing the keys to the bell-boy, and feeling only slightly less selfconscious, Joanna followed the man into the lift for the trip up to the third floor. She had already learned that Americans regarded the ground floor as the first floor, and consequently the fourth floor was in actual fact only three floors above the ground.

Her room overlooked the swimming pool at the back of the hotel. It was a large comfortable apartment, comprising a twin-bedded room with a balcony and an adjoining bathroom, and after the bell-boy had left her, Joanna walked out into the sunshine. Below her balcony, the water in the pool was alive with sunspots, while beyond the fringe of palms that edged the gardens, a narrow beach was all that separated the hotel from the Gulf of Mexico. It was exotic and it was colourful, and she rested her elbows on the rail and surveyed the activity below with a feeling of satisfation. She was here. She was actually here in Mango Key. All she had to do now was find Matthew Wilder.

All!

Screwing up her eyes against the glare, she acknowledged that it was no small task that Evan had set her. She had not been lying when she said that Uncle Matt might not recognise her. There was little resemblance now between the eight-year-old schoolgirl he had brought beads for and the nineteen-year-old young woman she had become. Indeed, she didn't remember him all that well. It was only the fact that her father had kept a photograph of Matthew Wilder in his study that had convinced her she might be able to recognise him. He couldn't have changed that much in eleven years. Her father hadn't. And after all, Uncle Matt was his contemporary, not hers.

On impulse, she went back into the room behind her and opened up her suitcase. She had brought the photograph with her, for reassurance, and now she drew it out and examined it once again. Marcia had made no bones about her taking any of the photographs out of her father's study. She had not wanted them, and after her father died, Joanna had gathered all the old snaps together and stuffed them into a holdall ready to sort through later. She was glad she had. The night she left Ashworth Terrace, she had been in no state to bother about old photographs, but because they had been among her possessions they had been sent to Mrs Morris's sister's house along with everything else she owned.

Now, she studied the old black and white image with faintly troubled eyes. The bearded features were familiar, and yet unfamiliar. She hardly remembered the man who had come back to England from Africa, bringing with him bracelets and necklaces carved from bone and shells, weird-looking dolls, and a pair of drums, wood-framed and covered with skin. It was all so long ago, and she felt the old sense of anxiety that he would immediately suspect why she was here.

The hollow feeling inside her resolved itself into hunger, and shedding the shorts for a more modest cotton wrap-around skirt, Joanna left her room and went down to the coffee shop. She had still to decide how she was going to arrange an accidental meeting with Matthew Wilder, and over a hamburger and french fries she considered the alternatives.

Evan had given her the address, along with the information that his house was near the beach. How Evan knew this, Joanna had no idea, but as the island was only three miles wide at its broadest point, it was not unreasonable to suppose that his information was correct. 'Palmetto Drive,' she mused, examining the slip of paper in front of her. It sounded nice, but names, like appearances, could be deceptive.

Still, at least she knew where to find him, always assuming he was still there. All she knew for certain was that he had been there six months ago or presumably her father would have changed the address in his diary.

Swallowing a mouthful of the raspberry milk shake she had ordered to accompany her hamburger, Joanna wiped her mouth on the back of her hand. There still remained the question of how she was going to introduce herself to a man who in all probability had even forgotten her name. How could she even get herself noticed when to all intents and purposes she was no different from any one of a thousand other girls she had seen thronging the beaches from here to Miami?

She was sitting there, lost in thought, when a light hand touched her shoulder. She glanced round at once, her long green eyes wide behind the curved lenses, and found the handsome young man from the reception desk regarding her with undisguised admiration.

'Miss Holland,' he said, as she met his gaze coolly, 'I thought you might be wondering about your car keys.' He smiled. 'Your car's been parked in the hotel garage. When you want it, all you have to do is call the desk and it'll be brought to reception for you.'

'Well, thank you.' Joanna couldn't be impolite. 'I'll remember that.'

'Good.' The young man hesitated. 'I hope your room is comfortable.'

'Oh, yes,' Joanna nodded. 'It's fine, really. Everything,' she included the coffee shop in the gesture she made, 'everything is fine—honestly.'

'That's good. If you have any problems, you tell me. Just ask for Carlos. Carlos Almeira, that's my name.'

Still he lingered, and Joanna, eager to get to grips with her own problems, felt a sense of impatience. What did he want, for goodness' sake? A written commendation? Or was he simply angling for a date? Either way, she was not interested.

'Was there something else?' she asked pointedly, waiting for him to leave her, and his tanned face creased into a smile.

'Do you know this area at all?' he enquired, confirming her worst fears, and she sighed.

'No. But I'll find my way around,' she averred coolly. 'G'bye.'

'Perhaps you'd like me to show you some of the tourist attractions,' he suggested, apparently immune to her indifference. 'We have quite a famous museum, down by the harbour, and a marine centre. And some of the architecture in the town dates from the turn of the century.'

'Thank you, but I prefer to do my own exploring,' replied Joanna crisply, and then caught her breath as a thought occurred to her. If—
Carlos—knew the town well, he would doubtless know who lived here, and also how far Palmetto Drive was from the hotel.

'Tell me,' she said, as he was turning away, and his philosophic expression gave way to one of anticipation. 'Yes?'

'I—is the island very big?' she asked, fingering the stem of her spectacles. 'I mean, could I walk from one end to the other?'

'You could,' conceded Carlos. 'But why walk when you have a car? It's too hot to walk. Except on to the beach.'

'I like walking,' said Joanna, tucking an errant strand of hair behind her ear. 'Besides, you see more that way.' She paused. 'I like to look at the names of the streets, to see if I recognise them. Some well-known people have lived on these islands from time to time. I suppose I'm just inquisitive.'

Carlos shrugged. 'No famous people live on Mango Key,' he declared, flattening her hopes in that direction. 'Key West now, that's different. That's where Ernest Hemingway used to live.'

'Yes, I know.' Joanna tried not to show her disappointment. 'I have read the guide books. I just thought you, being a local, might know of some interesting places.'

'Oh, I know a lot of interesting places,' declared Carlos, taking her innocent words as a sign of encouragement, and Joanna expelled her breath wearily.

'Thank you for your help,' she said, deliberately turning her head away, and with a gesture of impatience the young man left her.

Back in her room again, Joanna consulted her map. If Carlos had but known it, she knew exactly how big the island was, and running her finger along the coast from the hotel, she easily identified Palmetto Drive. It looked to be about half a mile from the hotel, and the tip of her tongue protruded between her lips as she considered what she should do. It was a hot afternoon, not at all the time of day any sensible person would choose to take a walk, but perhaps it was right for her purposes. She might even use it as a reason to gain entry to Matthew Wilder's house. A young woman, walking inadvisedly in the hot sun! An ideal way to effect an introduction. She could pretend she was lost, or she felt sick, or she was thirsty. Surely even a recluse would not deny her assistance!

She looked longingly down at the pool as she brushed her hair before re-coiling it into its knot. She would have liked nothing so much as to swim in the pool for a while, and then stretch out lazily in the sunshine, as other guests were doing. There was an air of somnolence about the hotel, and she hoped she was not being foolish by tempting a capricious fate. She really could get lost or be overcome by the heat, and she had no guarantee that the Uncle Matt she had known would come to her rescue.

She received a few speculative glances as she left the hotel. She had changed from the vest and wrap-around skirt into a silky yellow shirt, with elbow-length sleeves, and a pair of white culottes, and she felt horribly selfconscious at being alone. She was sure the eyes that followed her progress across the stretch of turf in front of the hotel would not have done so had she had an escort, and although she knew she was not unattractive, she came to the conclusion that any unattached female was regarded as fair game.

Palmetto Drive seemed further than she had anticipated. Or perhaps it was simply the heat and her increasing apprehension. It was all very well rehearsing what she was going to say in the quiet of her hotel room, and quite another to consider feigning surprise to a man who had so many years more experience.

Her route took her along Coral Reef Avenue,

and for a while she was enchanted by the creaming waters of the Gulf, surging on to the narrow beach on her right. A belt of palms separated the beach from the path, with here and there a sprawling mangrove tree, pushing up its roots through a tangle of marsh grass.

Across the street, an odd collection of shops and hotels jostled side by side. Fishing tackle and snorkelling equipment seemed to figure quite prominently, looking slightly out of place outside stores that had a distinctly mid-Western appearance, and small hotels, with latticed ironwork, boasted swimming pools and jacuzzis, which didn't quite fit their image.

Joanna would have liked to linger among the shops and stores, picking over the souvenirs available and maybe choosing herself a new book from the racks that seemed to occupy every available space. But putting off her objective wouldn't make it any the less inevitable, and ignoring the fluttery feeling in her stomach, she walked on.

Palmetto Drive appeared to be a continuation of Coral Reef Avenue, except that once the end of the avenue was reached, there were many fewer buildings. The populated part of the island swung away from the beach at this point, but a narrower road ploughed beneath a canopy of live oaks and the palmetto palms that gave it its name.

The houses, for there were no shops or hotels here, were set some distance from one another, and each stood in its own private grounds. In addition, they were on Joanna's right, forming a barrier between her and the beach, and the chance of invading anyone's privacy seemed unlikely indeed. It was also a little eerie walking along that

shadowy path, and Joanna didn't like the feeling
of intrusion it gave her.

The house she was looking for proved to be the
last in the line, and wrought-iron gates, securely
padlocked, shattered any hopes she might have
had of begging assistance. On the contrary, of all
the houses, it seemed the most remote, and peering
through the tall gates, she could see nothing but
flowering shrubs and trees. The foliage formed a
further screen to the house beyond, and its low
roof was all that was visible.

Sighing, Joanna turned back the way she had
come. Obviously she would have to think of
something else, but what? She could hardly ring
him up, could she? Although it might come to that
if she could think of nothing else. She shook her
head unhappily as she tramped back to the end of
the road, and then halted abruptly when she saw
the curve of the beach ahead of her. Of course—
why hadn't she thought of it before? The houses
backed on to the beach. It was worth taking a
walk along the shore, if only to assure herself that
the house was occupied.

Scrambling over the low wall that separated the
path from the tussocky grass that edged the beach,
she took off her sandals and allowed the grains of
sand to squeeze between her toes. It was very hot,
almost too hot for walking in places, so she
skipped down to the water's edge and walked
through the shallows. It would have been
enjoyable, had it not been for the sun beating
down on her head and shoulders, and she was glad
she was wearing a shirt, and not the sleeveless vest
she had worn earlier.

Nevertheless, she unbuttoned her shirt until
the dusky hollow between her breasts was visible,

and felt a trickle of moisture making its way down her spine. Even the slight breeze off the ocean made little headway in cooling her temperature, and she fanned herself apathetically as she progressed.

It took longer to walk along the beach. Apart from the fact that her feet were sucked down by the shifting sand, she had to negotiate a series of wooden breakwaters that intersected the sand in places. In addition to which, she had to watch out for crabs and sharp edges of coral, that could cause a nasty wound, as well as keeping an eye on the houses, to make sure she did not lose her bearings.

She was climbing over yet another wooden breakwater when the man accosted her. The sound of his voice, when she had thought she was alone, caused her to stub her foot on one of the wooden struts, and she gazed across at him indignantly, rubbing her injured toe.

'You're trespassing,' he declared, halting some distance from her and regarding her with hard aggressive eyes. 'The tourist areas are back the way you've come. I'm sorry, this is private property.'

Joanna pursed her lips. Apart from the fact that she was hot and tired, her toe was still stinging, and the realisation that this arrogant man was denying her her only chance of reaching Matthew Wilder's house made her behave more recklessly than she might have done.

'You should put up a sign,' she declared, stepping over the breakwater, and ignoring him she continued on along the beach.

'I said this is private property,' the man grated, taking the steps that put him squarely into her path. 'I'm sorry, but you can't go any further. Please—I must insist that you turn back.'

Joanna looked up at him mutinously. In spite of her height, he was taller than she was, and now that she had a chance to look at him properly, she couldn't help being aware of how attractive he was. He was about thirty-five, she estimated, brown skinned and tawny-eyed, with the lightest coloured hair she had seen on a man. It was a kind of ash-blond, she supposed, with a silvery sheen that was reflected in the bleached tips of short thick lashes. His nose was straight, his cheekbones high and slightly angular, and his mouth was thin and firm, above a determined jawline. Yet for all that, it was a sensual face, and she felt her senses stirring beneath his impatient gaze. He was wearing a pair of old denim shorts and a washed-out denim waistcoat, unbuttoned at present, and his skin was just as brown on his arms and legs as it was on his face. He was leanly built, but muscular, and judging from his manner, he was unused to being disobeyed.

'I'm sorry, too,' she said impulsively, wishing she could have met him on more friendly terms. 'I—er—I was just taking a walk. I wanted to get away from the tourist areas.'

'Really?' He sounded sceptical, and she thought rather crossly that he might have tried to meet her apology with some grace.

'Yes, really,' she insisted, feeling damp strands of hair clinging wetly to her neck. 'I only arrived on the island this morning, and I'm afraid I don't know my way around yet.'

'I see.'

The man inclined his head, but his eyes had taken on an oddly puzzled look. As if he was

speculating whether or not to believe her, thought
Joanna impatiently, feeling uncomfortably hot
standing there. The heat didn't seem to bother
him, but she was feeling decidedly thirsty, and she
longed rather desperately for a cool glass of Coke.

'I wonder——' she began, hesitating about how
best to frame her appeal, when the man's eyes
narrowed intently, and taking hold of her chin, he
turned her face into the sun.

Remembering with loathing the last time a
man had taken hold of her in this way, Joanna
should have recoiled from him. But this man's
hands were not Howard Rogers' hands; his fingers
were not hot or pudgy. They were long and strong
and cool, and Joanna knew the craziest urge to
cover his fingers with hers. Of course, she didn't,
but her green eyes turned up to his, unknowingly
provocative as they searched his lean dark face.

'Joanna,' he said suddenly, confounding all her
hopes and fears, and bringing a flush of confused
colour to her cheeks. 'My God, it is Joanna
Holland, isn't it? Or if it's not, you're her living
double!'

Joanna blinked. 'I—why, yes. Yes, I'm Joanna
Holland,' she got out jerkily. 'But how do you
know that? Who are you?'

Afterwards, she realised she had made exactly
the right response. Her voice had had precisely the
right inflection—that anxious note that fell
somewhere between interest and disbelief. But just
then she had had no thought of duplicity. On the
contrary, she was totally bewildered by the way he
suddenly let her go, stepping back from her
abruptly, as if afraid she might have some
contagion. In those first few seconds, she was
convinced she had never met this man before. If

she had she was sure she would not have forgotten, And only briefly, in the back of her mind, flickered the thought that he might have some connection with Matthew Wilder . . .

But as she recovered from the shock and her brain began to function again, reason came to her. Of course, she flayed herself impatiently, of course, that had to be the answer. After all, she was within a few yards of Matthew Wilder's house. She had let her attraction to the man blind her to the fact of her whereabouts, and for the moment she gave no thought to the question of how some colleague of the man she had come to find could identify her.

'Joanna,' he said again, incredulously now, pushing back his hair with a bewildered hand. The action parted the sides of the denim waistcoat, revealing the fine arrowing of hair that disappeared below the belt of his shorts and exposing an unexpectedly pale scar on the underside of his left arm. 'What the hell are you doing here?' His lips twisted. 'Don't tell me Marcia sent you!'

'Marcia?' Joanna could only stare at him, incapable of making any sense of this, and he expelled his breath resignedly.

'Marcia,' he repeated flatly. 'Marcia Stewart— she is your stepmother, isn't she?'

'Marcia Stewart married my father, yes,' answered Joanna unsteadily. 'But I don't understand——'

'Don't you remember me at all, Joanna?' he enquired, a trace of bitterness giving a cynical slant to his mouth. 'I'm Matthew Wilder. *Uncle* Matt, remember? Or have you forgotten that I ever existed?'

CHAPTER THREE

'You—you're Matthew Wilder!'

Joanna was stunned. She couldn't believe this *young*, disturbingly attractive individual was the man who had once carried her pick-a-back round her father's study. The Matthew Wilder she remembered was the Matthew Wilder from the photograph—a tall man, certainly, but much older and heavier built, with the bushy beard and moustache that had tickled her cheek when he kissed her.

'I guess you didn't know I lived out here,' he was saying now, interpreting her reaction as one of surprise at their encounter. 'I bought a house here about three years ago. I've made the island my home.'

Joanna shook her head, trying desperately to think of something suitable to say. But all she could think was that this was the man she had travelled so many thousands of miles to find, and it was all going to be so much easier than she had imagined.

'It's you,' she said at last. 'I thought—oh, I don't know, I thought you were older.'

'Did you think about me at all, Joanna?' he asked drily. 'I doubt it. A girl like you—you must live a very busy life.'

'Not so very,' answered Joanna, with a fleeting smile. 'Not like you. You were always on your way to some remote location or other. I used to envy you. Don't you find it dull now, living in the same place all the time?'

'No.' The syllable was clipped, and for a moment Joanna wondered if she had said something to offend him. But almost immediately, he added: 'I was very sorry to read about your father. You must miss him terribly. Still, I imagine you and Marcia are company for one another.' He paused. 'I suppose she's here with you.'

'No.' Joanna spoke hastily now, eager to dispel that particular illusion. It had been a surprise to learn that he appeared to know Marcia. She couldn't remember her stepmother ever mentioning him, or indeed her father ever discussing Matthew's activities with his wife. 'I—er—I'm on my own,' she went on, trying to sound casual. 'I'm nineteen now, you know. Not a little girl any more.' She smiled again. 'But it's lovely to see you again. Is that your house?'

She pointed to the sprawling villa just visible above a spiky wooden fence. Because the house was set on sloping ground, its pale cream walls were capable of being seen from this angle, and the profusion of plants and flowering shrubs that surrounded it only provided an exotic setting.

But if she had expected an invitation, she was disappointed. 'Yes,' he responded shortly, 'that's my house.' He gave her a polite smile in return. 'It's been a pleasure seeing you again, Joanna. But I'm afraid I must leave you now. I have work to do.' He half turned away. 'Enjoy the rest of your holiday——'

'Wait!' Joanna could not let him go like that. 'I mean——' this as he turned to her stiffly, his expression not so friendly now, more like the way it had been when he first found her trespassing, 'I wonder if I could trouble you for a drink?' She licked her dry lips expressively. 'It's such a hot afternoon, and I didn't realise I'd come so far. I'm staying at the Hotel Conchas, you see . . .'

Matthew's dark face mirrored his impatience, but common decency forbade his refusal. Even so, Joanna felt a sense of amazement that she had ever had the temerity to call him *Uncle* Matt. He seemed so remote now from the jolly playmate she remembered.

'A drink?' he said. 'Of what? Water? Lemonade?'

'Anything,' she averred. 'Water would do fine.' She grimaced. 'I'm sorry if I'm being a nuisance.'

He made no response to this, and she was left to the conclusion that she was being exactly that—a nuisance. He wasn't very friendly, she mused, wondering if her father had done anything to offend him before he died. But somehow she sensed his displeasure was not with her father, more with her, though what she had done to arouse it she couldn't honestly imagine. After all, he thought she had come upon him by accident. Heaven help her if he ever discovered the truth, she thought uneasily, following him across the sand to the iron gate set in the wooden fence.

'If you'd just wait here,' he said, astounding her still further, and she gazed at him aghast.

'Wait here?' she echoed. 'Can't I come with you?' She hesitated, and then decided she might as well plunge right in: 'I mean—I'd like to see your house, if you've no objection. It looks really beautiful!'

'But I do,' he interjected quietly. 'Have objections, that is. I'm afraid my home is off-limits to anyone. It's a little foible of mine. I permit no visitors.'

Joanna's cheeks flamed. 'I see.'

'I doubt you do, but I'll go and get your drink,' he remarked, swinging open the gate and mounting the first step. 'I'm sorry about this, Joanna, but believe me, it's for the best possible reasons.'

Joanna turned her back on him, but after a moment's sense of outrage she squatted down in the shade of the fence. It was such a relief to get out of the direct rays of the sun, and she blew her breath up over her face, enjoying the brief draught of air it afforded.

Matthew came back perhaps ten minutes later carrying a jug of iced fruit juice and a glass. 'Sorry to be so long,' he said, holding the glass out to her, and after she had taken it he filled it from the jug he was carrying. Joanna shook her head, still too affronted at his rudeness to offer him any respite. Instead she gulped thirstily at the delicious liquid, only pausing for breath when the glass was completely empty.

'Do you want some more?' he asked, but she made a barely audible refusal, her wet lips muffled against the back of her hand.

'I shouldn't like to detain you,' she declared, getting determinedly to her feet and brushing the sand from her culottes. Being submissive was going to get her nowhere, and she was disappointed that what she had thought was going to be so easy was proving to be so hard.

Matthew took the empty glass from her and set it, along with the jug, on the steps leading up through his garden. 'I'll walk with you to the breakwater,' he said, and although she was tempted to refuse him, she knew that giving in to pique would get her nowhere either.

'All right,' she said offhandedly, her mind

engrossed with the problem of how she was going to arrange another meeting, and he fell into step beside her, his hands pushed carelessly into the back pockets of his shorts.

'I suppose it surprises you that I recognised you,' he remarked, and briefly Joanna acknowledged that this was something she had not yet considered.

'How did you?' she asked, looking sideways at him, and his lips twisted humorously as he answered her question.

'From photographs,' he said simply. 'Your father wrote to me from time to time, and in his last letter he enclosed a picture of you. I believe it was taken after you'd won some art award. He was very proud of you.'

'Oh . . .' Joanna bent her head. 'It must have been the poster competition at school. I haven't won any other awards.'

'Nevertheless, you evidently have a talent in that direction.' Matthew paused. 'I gather you're not interested in writing.'

Joanna shrugged. 'Sometimes I think I would like to write children's books and illustrate them, but it's a very competitive field, and I don't think I'm good enough.'

'Are you sure you're not letting your father's success overshadow your own efforts?' he asked shrewdly. 'Perhaps you should discuss it with someone. What does—your stepmother say?'

'Marcia?' Joanna wondered how much to tell him. 'As a matter of fact, Marcia and I don't talk much any more.'

They had reached the breakwater, and she would have left him then, but now he detained her. 'What do you mean by that?' he asked, his attractive voice causing her to pause before scrambling over the wooden struts. 'Don't you and Marcia get on? Has there been some trouble between you since Drew died?'

'You might say that.' Even now, Joanna could feel her eyes smarting at the remembrance of what her father would say if he knew exactly what had happened. But pushing these thoughts aside, she politely held out her hand. 'Goodbye, Mr Wilder,' she said carefully. 'I hope we can meet again.'

He did not take her hand, however, and presently it fell, rather gauchely, to her side. He really was the most unpredictable man, she thought irritably, looking up at him through her lashes. But also the most disturbing, she conceded, aware of him as she had never been aware of any man before.

'Is that why you're here, holidaying alone?' he asked abruptly, apparently unwilling to abandon his theme. 'Have you and Marcia had a row? What's the matter? Didn't your father leave her enough?'

The note of irony in his voice was surprising, but Joanna was more concerned with the effect his words had on her. Until now, she had kept her thoughts about Marcia to herself, not even telling Sara Davenport, her best friend since their schooldays. But, unexpectedly, Matthew Wilder's enquiry struck a chord deep inside her, and she knew a sudden weakness to share her feelings with him.

Nevertheless, she stifled it. After all, this man was a virtual stranger to her, whatever his relationship with her father had been, and to confide in him now would be to give in to a purely emotional reflex.

'I'd better go,' she said, without answering him, shading her eyes against the glare of sun on sand. 'Thank you for the drink. It was delicious.'

Her companion inclined his head. 'It was my pleasure,' he responded drily, but she suspected he was only playing her game.

'Goodbye, then,' she said, not making the mistake of offering him her hand again, and he nodded.

'Goodbye, Joanna,' he replied, and by the time she had the temerity to look back, he had disappeared from sight.

Joanna awoke the next morning with a blinding headache. Her head had felt a bit muzzy when she went to bed, and she guessed it was her walk in the sun that was responsible for the present pounding in her temples. Feeling more than a little sorry for herself, she called room service and ordered toast and coffee, and while she was waiting for it to be delivered, she went into the bathroom and turned on the shower.

It didn't help when her telephone started ringing while she was standing under the abrasive spray. She hadn't bothered to put on a shower-cap and her long hair was soaking, but, half afraid that it might be Matthew Wilder, she wrapped a towel about herself and went to answer it.

Dripping water all over the bedside rug, she heard the operator ask her to hold on as she had a long-distance call for her. *Long-distance!* Joanna grimaced. It had to be Evan Price; no one else had any idea where she was.

'Joanna?' It was Evan, and she expelled her breath wearily as she heard his familiar tones.

'Hello, Evan,' she answered flatly. 'Look, is this

something urgent, because you've got me out of the shower.'

'You don't sound like a girl who's enjoying an unexpected winter vacation,' retorted Evan shortly, his voice echoing hollowly in her ear. 'I'm just ringing to find out what's going on. I haven't heard a squeak from you since you left England!'

'You may remember, I spent three days in Miami,' said Joanna defensively, and he snorted.

'I know that. Didn't I have to ring the hotel in Miami to find out where you were?' exclaimed Evan impatiently. 'You were supposed to keep me informed of your whereabouts, Joanna, not clear off without leaving me a forwarding address!'

'All right. I'm sorry.' Joanna sank down on to the side of the bed. 'But I only arrived here yesterday afternoon. I was going to ring you later today.'

'Hmm.' Evan sounded sceptical. 'Well? Have you anything to report?'

'After twenty-four hours?' Joanna protested, curiously loath to relate the events of the previous afternoon. 'Well, I do know where his house is.'

'You knew that before you left England,' said Evan dourly. 'Palmetto Drive, wasn't it? So what's new? Did you make a preliminary reconnaissance?'

Joanna gasped. 'You make it sound as if I'm spying on him!'

'Okay, okay.' Evan sounded a little less aggressive now. 'So you know where he lives. When are you going to see him?'

'When am I——? Evan, the house is practically impenetrable. It's surrounded by a high fence, and the gates are padlocked!'

'Yes. Yes, well, that's something you've got to

work out for yourself. That's what I'm paying you for, Joanna.'

'So it is.' Joanna couldn't keep the bitter note out of her voice. 'I just hope I can earn the money.'

'Joanna . . .' He sounded a little cajoling now, as if he realised he had gone too far. 'I've got every confidence in you. If anyone can do it, you can.'

'We'll see,' said Joanna, feeling an unwarranted stinging of tears behind her eyes. 'I—I'll ring you when I have any news. Goodbye.'

She rang off before he could say any more, guessing, correctly as it turned out, that he would not waste any more money ringing her again. So far as Evan was concerned she was here, she was following orders, and he wasn't really interested in anything but results.

Abandoning the shower, she dried herself thoroughly and was dressed in a dark red bikini and a matching wrap-around skirt when the man from room-service brought her breakfast. Thanking him, she carried the tray out on to the verandah, shady at present before the sun got round to this side of the hotel, and set it down on the spare lounger. Then, after pouring herself a cup of coffee, she subsided on to the other, swallowing a couple of aspirin she had taken from her bag.

The view was magnificent, but she was in no real mood to appreciate it. She felt guilty on two counts: one, because she had let Matthew Wilder believe she was as surprised to see him as he had been to see her, and two, because she had withheld the information from Evan. Her feelings didn't improve her headache, and she closed her eyes wearily, longing for inspiration.

After she had swallowed a little of the toast, the pounding in her head had eased a little, and realising the maid would be waiting to come and clean the room, Joanna collected her bag and a paperback novel and went downstairs. She found a shaded corner of the sun-deck, and ignoring the sensation that she was the only solitary holiday-maker there, she tried to forget her problems for the morning at least. There was plenty to see if she chose not to read. The pool was the magnet for all the children staying in the hotel, and their parents stretched out in the sunshine, content to oil their bodies and leave their offspring to their own devices.

By the time the sun got round to Joanna's particular corner, she was ready for a swim herself, but leaving the pool to the young ones, she crossed the beach and took her first plunge into the sparkling waters of the Gulf. For almost half an hour she determinedly ignored the reason that had brought her to Mango Key, and revelled in the simple delight of feeling sun-warmed water cooling her hot skin.

It was lunchtime when she came back to her chair to towel herself dry. Already several people had deserted the sun-deck in search of food, and it was quieter now that many of the children had left with their parents. Aware that her bikini-clad figure was attracting the attention of indolent male eyes, Joanna collected her bag, book and spectacles, and sliding the glasses on to her nose, she made for the hotel. It wasn't always easy to deter a dogged suitor, and the last thing she needed right now were complications of that kind.

She ate lunch in the coffee shop, as on the previous afternoon, and then returned to her room to try and plan some strategy. The trouble was, there seemed no way she could arrange to meet Matthew Wilder accidentally, and although their encounter on the beach had seemed a heaven-sent opportunity, in retrospect she had to admit she had not gained any advantage. She should have realised that after living the life of a recluse for almost three years he was unlikely to take kindly to any intrusion into his privacy and, short of appealing to the respect he had had for her father, she could see no way of developing their association.

If only he had invited her into his house! Then she could have presumed on that relationship to call again, and surely during their conversations she could have found out what Evan wanted to know. His main objective seemed to be to discover what Matthew Wilder had been doing for the past three years, and why he had abandoned his research work at the London institute. He had shown no particular interest in the man's private life, for which Joanna was grateful. Her conscience was troubling her because she had agreed to pry into Matthew Wilder's professional activities; how much worse she would have felt if Evan had asked her to conduct some kind of personal investigation.

She left the hotel in the late afternoon, when the sun had lost most of its heat, and it was possible to walk without getting exhausted. But she didn't go as far as Palmetto Drive, even though she wished she could. Instead, she visited the shops along Coral Reef Avenue, that she had seen the previous afternoon, buying herself some sun-tan lotion and various other personal items she could not get in the hotel.

The sea was a burnished shade of amber as she walked back to the hotel. She had never seen the water quite that colour before, and she paused for a few minutes to enjoy its beauty. With the sun sinking lower every minute, its dying rays were spreading fingers of gold into the darkening sky, and here and there a star glittered, already eager to take its place.

It was a heavenly spot, she thought dreamily, envying anyone who could make their home here. Matthew had chosen an ideal place to make his retreat. No wonder he shunned publicity! Half the island's charm was its remote inaccessibility. But why had he cut himself off from the world? she wondered, unable to deny her curiosity. Had something happened to disillusion him? Had one of his experiments gone wrong? Her father had told her once that 'Uncle' Matt's work was mostly concerned with tropical diseases. Had a mistake been made for which he blamed himself, or was it simply that he had equipped a private laboratory, and was conducting some research of his own? Somehow, she was expected to find out—and without betraying her interest.

She sighed. If only he had been more like the man she remembered, older—the avuncular figure she had expected him to be. The man she now knew as Matthew Wilder was too young to be regarded as an uncle, and much too elusive for her to try any other approach. Obviously, he had no desire to expand their acquaintance, or he would have relaxed his carefully-guarded privacy and allowed her into his house. So far as he was concerned, she was just the daughter of an old friend, whose death had severed their connection. Just because she had found him physically attractive——

'Carry your bag, lady?'

The teasing voice brought Joanna round, almost guiltily, aware that her thoughts at that moment did not bear exposure. 'What? Oh——' her lips drooped disconsolately as she recognised one of the young men who had been on the sun-deck that morning. 'I beg your pardon?'

'You looked lonely,' the young man declared, unabashed by her cool enquiry. 'If you're walking back to the hotel, I'll join you.'

'Thank you, that won't be necessary,' said Joanna, at her most aloof, and ignoring his startled face, she set off at a brisk pace. But to her annoyance, he only let her get a few yards ahead before catching up with her, pushing his hands into the pockets of his jeans, and giving her a curious sideways glance.

'Did I say something?' he asked, and she recognised his accent as coming from the north-eastern corner of the United States. 'Look, I'm only trying to be friendly. You seem to be on your own, okay? I thought you might be glad of some company.'

'Did you?' Joanna did not ease her pace, and he lifted his shoulders appeasingly.

'I guess you're used to guys like me,' he remarked ruefully. 'A girl like you, you've got to be waiting for somebody, right?'

Joanna sighed. 'Something like that,' she agreed, and then relented. After all, it wasn't in her nature to be rude to anyone without just cause, and while she wanted to avoid complications of this sort, he was a good-looking boy and she couldn't help feeling flattered that he should have singled her out. 'I'm just not very good company at the moment.'

'You're from England, aren't you?' he asked. 'Is this your first visit to the States?'

'It's my first visit to Florida,' amended Joanna. 'I came to the United States some years ago with my father. And yes,' she smiled at his anticipatory features, 'I am enjoying my holiday. It really is a beautiful part of the world.'

'So how long are you staying?' he persisted, following her into the hotel foyer. 'My name's Tom Connolly, by the way. What's yours?'

'Don't push your luck,' murmured Joanna drily, softening her remark with a smile. 'Goodbye, Mr Connolly. Thank you for your escort.'

He looked decidedly crestfallen at the abruptness of her dismissal, but aware that Carlos Almeira was on duty at the desk, Joanna had no wish to encourage him to think that she was easy game.

Before she could escape into the lift, however, Carlos called her name. 'Miss Holland,' he said, making it impossible for Tom Connolly not to hear, 'do you have a minute, please?'

Joanna sighed, and giving up the attempt to make a hasty getaway, she walked resignedly back to the desk. 'Yes?'

'There's a message for you, Miss Holland,' Carlos stated importantly, and Joanna's heart raced. A message? From whom? Then her pulse rate subsided. It was probably Evan Price again.

'What is it?' she asked, keeping her tone carefully neutral, and aware of Tom Connolly behind her, eager to hear what the message was, she hoped Carlos would be discreet.

'A—Mr Wilder called,' he said, producing a slip of paper from her slot in the letter rack. 'He left his number and asked if you would call him back.'

CHAPTER FOUR

JOANNA prepared for dinner the following evening in nervous anticipation. It was important that she didn't waste this heaven-sent opportunity, and she had spent the day rehearsing what she was going to say: *'How lucky you are to live in such a heavenly place, Mr Wilder! I don't suppose you'll ever want to go back to England. But don't you ever feel isolated from the people you used to work with? Are you working at present——'*

At this point, her nerve generally gave out on her, and as she stroked a gold mascara across the skin above her eyelids, the brush shook a little. This invitation had been so incredible, so unexpected, after all, and she was only now absorbing the fact that Matthew Wilder had invited her to dinner; not to some impersonal restaurant, to his house on Palmetto Drive—and she was terrified.

The previous evening she had had the operator connect her with his house firmly convinced that somehow he had discovered her real purpose for being on Mango Key. She had been quite prepared for him to bawl her out, to castigate her for her deceit, and tell her to keep away from his property. But he hadn't. He had been courtesy itself, and his casual invitation to dinner had left her a trembling wreck.

'To—to dinner?' she had stammered disbelievingly, and he had said yes, he would like her to join him for dinner at his home.

'At your house?' she had echoed, scarcely capable of taking it in, and he assured her that that was what he wanted. 'But you said you never had any visitors,' she had protested, a statement that afterwards she had been horrified at herself for uttering, but once again it had proved providential.

'I'm prepared to make an exception for Drew's daughter,' he had replied, his low voice stirring her emotions. 'Take a cab. I'll expect you about eight.'

Joanna had hardly slept that night. Even though her bed was superbly comfortable, she couldn't get comfortable in it, and at first light she was down in the pool, enjoying its cold refreshing isolation. She had breakfasted in the coffee shop, surprising the waitress by ordering strawberry pancakes, and afterwards she had gone shopping, unable to control the equal waves of excitement and fear that were rising inside her. She knew why she was excited; she didn't know why she was afraid. But one thing was certain, she couldn't relax, and by the time darkness fell, she was in a rare state of trepidation.

Finishing her make-up now, she turned to take the outfit she had chosen to wear from its hanger. It was a tunic of wine silk jersey, worn with matching trousers that clung to her shapely legs. The neck of the tunic was low and square, and its straight lines drew attention to the pointed swell of Joanna's firm breasts. With it she wore a long gold chain, looped twice around her throat and allowed to hang almost to her waist, and a matching bracelet. Her long hair was coiled into a sleek chignon, and examining her appearance, she was satisfied that tonight Matthew could not mistake her for a schoolgirl.

To her relief, Carlos was not at the reception desk when she walked into the foyer of the hotel, and the young female who had taken his place paid her only the briefest of attention.

'There's a cab out front,' she declared laconically, when Joanna asked if she would summon her one, and flicking her clutch bag against her thigh, Joanna crossed to the revolving glass doors.

There were several people about, but happily no one she recognised, and the cab driver waiting outside was too used to driving glamorous people around to pay much attention to his current passenger. However, when she gave him the address, he did show a trace of interest.

'Palmetto Drive,' he echoed, switching off his 'For Hire' sign. 'You sure that's where you want to go?'

'I'm sure,' she said, settling rather nervously into the back. 'You do know where it is, don't you?'

'Oh, yeah, I know where it is,' agreed the driver drily. 'Just don't get many people from the hotel visiting the folks who live along Palmetto Drive, is all.'

'Oh.' Joanna tried not to be inquisitive, but she couldn't help asking: 'Why not?'

'Expensive houses along Palmetto Drive,' remarked the driver sagely. 'That's where the rich folks live. You seen them houses, have you? Some of them are worth over a million dollars!'

'Really?' Joanna was impressed. 'I didn't know that.'

'Huh!' The driver grimaced into the rear-view mirror as they pulled away from the hotel. 'I guess you're from England, aren't you? You'll be used to expensive houses maybe.'

'Not really,' said Joanna uneasily, wondering what she was letting herself in for, and was glad when the necessity to negotiate the traffic distracted the driver's attention.

Palmetto Drive looked even more eerie at night. There were no lights along the avenue, and only the lights beyond the high walls revealed that the houses were inhabited.

'It's right at the far end,' she said, leaning forward in her seat as the cab-driver slowed to look for Number Fifteen. 'I—er—this will do fine, thank you.'

'You sure they know you're coming?' asked the driver, his voice revealing an unexpected note of concern, and Joanna forced a smile.

'Oh, they know,' she assured him firmly, and climbing out of the cab, she paid him his fare. 'Thank you.'

'I'll wait until you get inside,' the driver told her gruffly, looking past her at the tall iron gates. 'You want I should blow my horn? Don't seem like they've heard you.'

Joanna hesitated, and then, observing an iron bell-pull beside the gate, she tugged on it. 'Really,' she said, 'I'll be fine, thank you.' The last thing she wanted was for Matthew Wilder to think she was nervous, even if she was. 'Goodbye.'

The driver shrugged, but he had to turn his cab around, and by the time he had done so, a light had come on above the gate, and Joanna could hear footsteps.

It was not Matthew Wilder, however, who opened the gate to her. It was, surprisingly enough, a woman; a woman of about thirty, moreover, with tightly curled hair, hennaed to a surprising shade of red, dark brown eyes, and a magnolia-pale sultry beauty. She was wearing an apron over a green cotton dress, and her heavy breasts pressed voluptuously against the material. However, the look she directed at Joanna was not friendly, and the girl wondered fleetingly if she had come to the right place.

'I—er—I'm Joanna Holland,' she volunteered, half hoping she had made a mistake, but the woman held the gate wide and invited her in, which seemed to conclude the matter.

After making sure the gate was securely locked again the woman led the way along a path between tall vine-covered trellises. She had evidently switched on some kind of floodlighting before leaving the house, and now Joanna could see her way quite clearly—which was just as well, as her escort said nothing at all.

She guessed the gardens would be a blaze of colour in daylight, but in the artificial lighting it was possible to identify the blossoms of a more temperate climate vying with pale magnolias and waxen camellias and delicately tinted orchids. There were smooth stretches of grass, and a stone-edged lily pond, and a hedge of flowering acacia, its fragrant yellow flowers scenting the air with their sweetness. But it was the house itself that inspired most interest, and now that she could see it, Joanna stared unashamedly.

Matthew Wilder's tropical retreat bore little resemblance to a hermitage. It was a sprawling white-painted villa, with bougainvillea hanging over the porch and around the shuttered windows, and a sloping tile roof behind a screen of sturdy palms. It was presently lit by half a dozen angled spotlights, and seeing it for the first time, Joanna couldn't help the tiny gasp of admiration that escaped her. It was such a beautiful house, and understandably worthy of protection.

She followed the woman into the house across a verandah where alabaster urns spilled scarlet geraniums over fluted wooden rails. They entered an oblong hall, tiled in squares of black and white, and illuminated by wall lamps that cast prisms of light over white-panelled walls. There was nothing in the hall but a circular glass-topped table, on which was set a squat bronze bowl filled with dark red Mariposa lilies. Dimly-lit passages led away to left and right, and immediately ahead of them, two shallow steps led down into an elegantly-furnished living room.

'Wait here,' ordered the woman curtly before sauntering off along one of the passages. Joanna watched the deliberate sway of the woman's hips as her back was presented to her, and then she turned a corner and disappeared from view.

Clasping her bag with both hands, Joanna endeavoured to sustain her interest in her surroundings, but now that she was here, her overriding concern was that she should not make any mistakes. Already she had been mistaken in thinking Matthew Wilder lived here alone. Evidently the woman who had escorted her from the gate lived here, too, and while her apron had led Joanna to believe she must be a servant, her attitude had not. Exactly what position did she hold? What might her relationship to Matthew Wilder be? The most obvious one was unpalatable, but what did she really know about the man who had been her father's friend?

'Joanna.'

She had been so lost in thought, she had not heard his approach, and she started at the sound of his voice. He crossed the hall towards her, moving with lithe, purposeful steps, and she expelled her breath nervously as he offered a polite smile.

'I'm sorry if I've kept you waiting,' he said, gesturing towards the steps that led down into the living room. 'Won't you join me? We can have a drink before the meal.'

Joanna nodded, moving ahead of him jerkily, intensely conscious of him at her back. This evening he was a black panther, she thought imaginatively. If, when she met him on the beach, he had been all sleek-skinned and tawny gold, like a lion, this evening he resembled a different member of the cat family. His black ruffled evening shirt hid the pelt of sun-bleached hair that had roughened the skin of his body, and the tight-fitting black pants only hinted at the powerful muscles of his thighs. He wore no jacket, just a narrow strip of black leather, tied in a bow at his throat, that like the rest of his attire threw the amazing lightness of his hair into stark relief.

In an effort to break the spell of his attraction, Joanna gave her attention to the room they were entering. It was a large room, tastefully designed, but comfortable, with long velvet-covered sofas, and cabinets containing an assortment of items, from exquisite porcelain figurines to rather frightening-looking African masks. There were bookshelves beside a veined-stone fireplace, where a pile of logs could be kindled on cold evenings, and lots of pictures on the plain walls, giving them warmth and light and colour. The illumination came from tall lamps and smaller ones, set behind the sofa and on the bookshelves, casting a mellow glow over everything.

'What—what a lovely room!' exclaimed Joanna, speaking for the first time, and Matthew inclined his head.

'I like it,' he affirmed, indicating that she should take a seat on one of the cream velvet sofas. 'Now, what will you drink? Martini? Sherry? Coke?'

Joanna suppressed the urge to assert the fact that she was nineteen and not *nine*, and accepted a dry sherry. Matthew poured himself a Scotch and soda, she noticed, and then came to sit opposite her, on the other sofa.

'So,' he said, spreading his legs wide and holding his glass suspended between, 'are you still enjoying your holiday?'

'Oh—yes.' Joanna pressed her knees tightly together and raised her glass to her lips for protection. 'The—er—the hotel is very good, and the weather's been glorious so far.'

'It generally is, at this time of the year,' Matthew stated flatly. 'Later on, it becomes more humid, but right now it's just about perfect.'

'Yes.' Joanna sipped her sherry a little nervously, and pushed her spectacles up her nose. The weather might not feel humid to him, but her skin felt moist, and she hoped her nose did not look as slippery as it felt.

'You've always worn glasses, haven't you?' he said suddenly, and Joanna looked across at him.

'You remember?'

'Oh, yes. I remember a little girl in pigtails wearing horn-rimmed spectacles, who used to ask what I'd brought her every time I came back from some trip or other.'

'Did I do that?' Joanna was appalled. 'I—I do recall certain things you brought me. A—a drum, and a bracelet; oh, yes, and some beads.'

Matthew looked down into his glass. 'It seems a long time ago,' he said, half to himself, and Joanna quickly agreed with him.

'It *was* a long time ago. Eleven years, to be exact,' she declared staunchly. 'I'm not a little girl any longer.'

'No, you're not.' Matthew conceded the point almost ruefully. 'You make me feel very old.'

'You're not old.' Joanna spoke recklessly. 'You're much younger than I had expected—I mean,' this as she realised exactly what she was saying, 'I told you, I—I always imagined you were Daddy's age.'

'I am.'

Joanna's brows descended. 'Daddy was forty-five when he died. You're not forty-five!

'I'm forty,' he told her mildly. 'Or I shall be in October. Old enough to be your father, I think you'll agree.'

Joanna shook her head. 'You don't look it.'

'Well, thank you, but I feel it. Most of the time, anyway.'

'Is that why you left England?' asked Joanna impulsively. 'Because you felt you needed a—a rest?'

There was a brief silence, when Joanna wondered whether she had said too much. But then Matthew finished his Scotch and putting the glass aside, said: 'I didn't bring you here to talk about me, Joanna. I wanted to talk about you. I want to know what you're doing out here on your own, while Marcia is apparently neglecting her responsibilities in London.'

The reappearance of the woman who had let Joanna into the villa prevented her from answering. Much to Joanna's relief, she appeared at the head of the steps leading down into the living room, and announced in husky tones that dinner was waiting.

'Thank you, Elena.' Matthew got up from the sofa and smiled at her. 'By the way, have you two introduced yourselves? Joanna Holland—Elena Massey. Elena is my—housekeeper.'

His hesitation before uttering the last word was not lost on Joanna, and she was unable to prevent her features from stiffening as she rose to her feet to accompany him. 'How do you do, Miss Massey,' she murmured, forcing herself to be polite, and the other woman's lips twisted knowingly as she exchanged a glance with her employer.

'It's *Mrs* Massey, actually, Miss Holland,' she corrected, her accent unrecognisable to Joanna. 'It's very nice to meet you, I'm sure. Now, if you'll excuse me . . .'

Joanna did not look at Matthew as they mounted the steps and followed Elena Massey's seductively swaying form along the corridor. She was too busy trying to assimilate two facts: one, that Matthew had brought her here, apparently with some idea of reassuring himself as to her welfare, and two, that far from living the life of a recluse, he had the sensual charms of Elena Massey to console him.

Dinner was served in an attractively furnished dining room. It was not a large room, but the rectangular table would have seated six people comfortably, and several handwoven tapestries added colour to its cream-washed walls.

The meal was plain but delicious. A seafood chowder was followed by barbecued spare ribs, served on a bed of fluffy rice, and to finish there was the Key lime pie, which Joanna had already tasted at the hotel. Elena brought the dishes to the table, but she left them to serve themselves, and Joanna was grateful not to have to eat too much.

She noticed that Matthew didn't eat a lot either, nor did he partake too freely of the bottle of white wine standing in an ice-bucket beside him. He seemed somewhat pensive throughout the meal, and because Elena was coming backwards and forwards, he did not broach the subject of Joanna's situation until they returned to the living room to have coffee.

But once the cups had been attended to, and Elena had withdrawn, he subjected Joanna to a rather brooding appraisal. 'Tell me,' he said without preamble, 'didn't your father ever tell you it was dangerous to travel so far alone? I can't imagine what Marcia was thinking of. Doesn't she have any control over the way you spend your money?'

'I don't have any money,' replied Joanna, setting her coffee cup aside, and then realising belatedly how this could be misconstrued, she added: 'Well, not a lot, anyway.'

Matthew frowned. 'I don't understand. Your father was a wealthy man.'

'Yes.' Joanna moistened her lips. 'But he didn't leave a will.'

Matthew, who had been watching her through narrowed lids like some dark avenging angel, now abandoned his side of the hearth to come and take the seat beside her, 'What's that supposed to mean?' he demanded, his tawny eyes hard and intent. 'What's happened?'

'Nothing much,' Joanna shrugged, bending her head a little nervously as she felt his breath fan her neck. 'Just—well, Marcia controls our financial affairs, that's all.'

'You mean *her* financial affairs, don't you?' corrected Matthew tautly. 'What are you saying? That she's commandeered the major part of your father's estate?'

'Something like that.'

Matthew let out his breath heavily. 'Drew always was a fool where she was concerned,' he muttered, and then offered an unwilling apology. 'I'm sorry. But I feel pretty bad about this.' He paused. 'So—what are you going to do about it?'

'What can I do?' asked Joanna helplessly, turning to look at him, only to draw in her breath abruptly as she encountered his impatient gaze only a few inches from her face.

She guessed from the instinctive way he drew back from her that he had not intended to get so close, but it was too late now to avoid it. Briefly, their eyes met and held, translucent green on smouldering gold, and in those emotionally-charged seconds, Joanna sensed the sudden change in the atmosphere. Then, with a controlled movement, he got to his feet and put the width of the room between them, leaving her with the shaky conviction that once again she had wasted her opportunities.

'Can I offer you another drink before you go?' he asked, his voice as cool and detached as it had been on her arrival, and Joanna expelled the breath she had been holding and nodded jerkily.

'Scotch, please,' she said, causing him to glance half impatiently round at her. 'Just to prove I'm not as helpless as you think.'

Matthew shrugged. 'I don't think you're helpless, just—ill-advised. The last thing someone of your precarious financial status should be doing is taking a holiday in Florida! You should be in contact with your father's solicitor, arranging with him to make some sort of settlement.'

'Oh, yes.' Joanna took the glass he proffered rather cynically. 'Well, that's another story. Right now——' she looked up at him deliberately, 'right now, I needed a break.'

Matthew shook his head, moving back to pour himself a drink. 'You know your own situation best, I suppose,' he said levelly. 'What made you choose Florida?'

'Oh—I——' Joanna could feel the colour invading her cheeks, and the knowledge that she could only lie to him made her feel worse. 'It—it was somewhere I wanted to see.' She paused, before adding recklessly: 'I'm glad it was.'

Matthew made no response to this other than finishing his drink, setting down his glass, and walking purposefully across the room. 'I'll go call you a cab,' he said, reaching the steps, and his brusque tone alerted her to the fact that the evening was almost over and he had learned more about her than she had about him.

'Couldn't—couldn't you take me home?' she asked daringly, getting up. 'I mean, you do have a car, don't you?'

'Yes, I have a car,' agreed Matthew shortly. 'But I seldom drive, and as you came in a cab, surely you can go back that way.'

'Well, yes. But it is late,' said Joanna lamely, glancing surreptitiously at her watch. It was after ten o'clock, which could hardly be considered late by island standards, but he was not to know how late it was for her. 'And I am on my own, as you pointed out.'

Matthew sighed, his mouth turning down at the corners. 'Very well,' he said, after subjecting her to a minute scrutiny. 'If you feel that way, I have no alternative. If you'll excuse me a moment, I'll get the car.'

It was waiting at the gate as they walked through the gardens to the road. Now that Joanna had an opportunity to get her bearings, she could see the drive that ran parallel to the path, and the flat-roofed garage to one side of the villa.

The car was an American limousine, sleek-lined, but dusty, evidently after spending its days in the garage. Even so, it was a definite improvement on the cab that had brought her to the villa, and she settled into the front seat comfortably, watching Matthew coil his lean length beside her.

'I—why don't you do much driving?' she asked, as he started the engine, realising she would have to accelerate her plans if she wanted to get to know anything. 'Don't you ever leave the island? Or do you generally fly everywhere you need to go?'

'I don't leave the island,' answered Matthew flatly, concentrating on the road ahead. 'I have most things I need here. If I do need anything else, I send for it.'

Joanna shook her head. 'But don't you miss England? I mean, I know Florida's a beautiful state, but——'

'I don't miss England,' stated Matthew brusquely. 'Nor do I wish to go back. I've just told you, I have everything I need here. Now do you mind if we change the subject?'

Joanna moistened her lips. 'But your work——' She broke off unhappily. 'Don't you miss your work? Or are you working here?'

'What is this?' Matthew glanced sideways at her as they emerged from the shadows of Palmetto Drive into the floodlit brilliance of Coral Reef Avenue. 'What do you know about my work? Did your father talk to you about it?'

Joanna flushed. 'Why, no. No, not really. He said you used to have something to do with tropical medicine, but that's all. I—I was just interested ...'

'Forget it,' said Matthew, allowing the car to pick up speed along the brightly-lit thoroughfare. 'Just accept the fact that I'm not in circulation any more.' His lips twisted. 'Yes, that's it. I've dropped out of circulation, right?' He made a bitter sound. 'And you'll never know just how accurate that is!'

CHAPTER FIVE

Two days later, Evan rang.

Joanna had spent the time since the night she had had dinner at Matthew Wilder's house trying to come up with some reason why she might contact him again, and Evan's call made her guiltily aware that she was no longer acting on his behalf. On the contrary, her reasons for wanting to see Matthew again were wholly personal—which was quite ridiculous, she acknowledged, considering how little encouragement he had given her. He had dropped her at her hotel without making any arrangement to see her again, and she had been left with the distinct impression that so far as Matthew Wilder was concerned she could only be a nuisance.

Nevertheless, it wasn't so easy to put him out of her mind. He was the first thing she thought of when she woke up in the morning, and the last fleeting image before she fell asleep. Not that she was sleeping awfully well. She was plagued with dreams of Elena Massey, her voluptuous figure always evident in various stages of undress, floating through the rooms of Matthew's house, inviting him to make love to her. Joanna's dreams generally stopped short of the actual act, inexperience proving a stumbling block even subconsciously; but that didn't prevent her from imagining what happened, and pictures of Matthew's lean sinuous body entwined with that of his housekeeper brought Joanna out of her shallow oblivion to lie sleepless through the early morning hours.

Evan rang as she was finishing her lunch in the coffee shop, and hearing her name paged, Joanna knew a wild hope that it might be Matthew. But taking the call in one of the perspex kiosks in the foyer she quickly discovered that she was mistaken, and as before, Evan sounded rather irate.

'Don't tell me you haven't seen him yet!' was his opening accusation, and Joanna propped herself against the wall beside the phone, welcoming the cool plaster against her hot back.

'I—no,' she said at last, unwillingly. 'I'm not going to tell you I haven't seen him, but I have nothing to report.'

'What do you mean, you have nothing to report?' snapped the publisher. 'Joanna, if you've seen Wilder, you must have spoken to him. If you're holding out on me——'

Joanna moistened her upper lip. 'I'm not—holding out on you, Evan,' she protested uncomfortably. 'I told you I'd ring if I had anything to tell you. I don't. I know no more now than I did before I left England.'

'What the hell is that supposed to mean? Are you telling me you've spoken to him without asking him what he's doing?'

'Evan!' Joanna felt justifiably indignant now. 'What do you want me to do? Present him with a questionnaire? Sort of—fill that out and return it to me at your earliest convenience?'

'Don't talk down to me, Joanna. You know what I mean. But I want some answers.'

'Don't we all,' retorted Joanna stiffly. 'I'm sorry, Evan, but I can't work like that. I—I've seen him, I've spoken to him; I—I've even had dinner with him——'

'Dinner!' exclaimed Evan, his tone altering considerably. 'You've actually had dinner with him, Joanna? Where?'

'At—at his house,' muttered Joanna reluctantly, already regretting betraying the information. 'But you can't rush these things, Evan. I—he's going to get suspicious if I start asking too many personal questions all at once——'

'Sure he is, sure he is.' From Evan's attitude now, it was obvious he was revising his previous opinion, and when he spoke again there was a pitch of excitement in his voice: 'I can't believe this, Joanna. You've actually done it! You've actually got into his house! Do you realise how important this is?'

'I think so.' Joanna hesitated. 'But it means nothing. I—I don't know any more about him, honestly. He—he wouldn't talk about himself at all.'

'He will. He will.' Evan sounded supremely confident. 'A man like that, cut off from all his friends and colleagues; sooner or later he's bound to confide in you, Joanna. You're his best friend's daughter, the little girl he used to dandle on his knee——'

'Hardly that, Evan!'

'Nevertheless, you're there, you're a reminder of his past. It's only human nature for a man to want to unburden himself to somebody——'

'He's not alone, Evan,' put in Joanna flatly. 'There—there's a woman. His housekeeper, a Mrs Massey.'

'Massey, did you say?' Evan made a thoughtful sound. 'I'll check it out. No problem. So—when are you seeing Wilder again?'

'I'm not.' Joanna was offhand.

'What do you mean, you're not?' Evan was evidently trying not to lose his temper again. 'Joanna, don't tease me, please. I realise you're doing a good job there, but don't play games with me.'

'I'm not playing games with you, Evan,' averred Joanna, with a sigh. 'We had dinner, yes, but I think that was only for old times' sake, as you say. He felt—sorry for me.'

'Sorry for you?'

'Yes.' Joanna paused. 'He asked about—about Daddy getting killed and how Marcia had reacted.'

'So you told him?'

'Some of it, yes.'

'Brilliant!' Evan was enthusiastic. 'You really know how to pull the sympathy.'

'That wasn't my intention.' Joanna was indignant. 'Evan, I didn't——'

'But that's what makes it so perfect, don't you see?' Evan interrupted her impatiently. 'You're a natural, Joanna, you really are. Hell, I bet you had the poor guy weeping into his soup!'

Joanna wished she had never started this. 'I think you're horrible!' she declared, wishing she could hang up on him. 'It wasn't like that. I don't need anyone's sympathy. I'm quite capable of handling my own life.'

'Okay, okay.' Evan stifled his triumphant laughter. 'Just keep up the good work, that's all. You'll think of something.'

'I may not.' Joanna was mutinous. 'I may just catch the next flight home.'

'You wouldn't do that.' Evan spoke with conviction. 'I mean, if you did, you'd ruin everything, wouldn't you? You can't expect me to foot your hotel bills or pay your fare if you don't deliver the goods. And just think what a hole that will make in your bank balance!'

'But——' Joanna glanced surreptitiously behind her, assuring herself that no one was within hearing distance, 'what about the five thousand pounds you promised to pay me?'

'I pay on results, Joanna, you should know that. If you hadn't had any success, if Wilder had refused to see you—well, I guess I'd have had to pay up. I'm not unreasonable, Joanna. But I'm not a philanthropist, either, and we both know you can do this, if you really set your mind to it.'

Joanna's fingers hurt as they gripped the phone. 'That—that's not fair,' she choked, but Evan was not listening to her.

'I'll look forward to hearing from you, Joanna,' he said, pleasantly. 'Have a nice day.'

Joanna was still leaning against the wall beside the phone when Tom Connolly sauntered out of the lift. His eyes brightened perceptibly when he saw her, and much to her regret he strolled towards her.

'Hi,' he greeted her irrepressibly, arching a questioning brow. 'You look like you had some bad news.' He halted in front of her. 'Has he let you down?'

Joanna let out her breath unsteadily. 'In a manner of speaking,' she said, straightening away from the wall. 'If you'll excuse me . . .'

'Hey, don't be like that!' Tom adopted a wounded expression. 'Can I help it if your old man has decided business is more important than pleasure? Come on, give me a break. I'm going windsurfing this afternoon. Why don't you join me?'

'I don't think so.' Joanna tried to soften her refusal with a smile. 'I don't feel much like windsurfing right now. I think I'll go up to my room.'

'Well, hey, I'd come with you, if you'd let me,' declared Tom, grinning. 'What floor is your room on? Let me guess—the fourth?'

Joanna edged her way out of the kiosk, shaking her head. 'Nice try,' she complimented him drily, feeling a little less raw than she had done a few moments ago. 'Enjoy your afternoon. I may see you from my balcony.'

'Is that a promise?' Tom accompanied her to the lift. 'Aren't you afraid I'll find out where your room is—Joanna?'

Joanna sighed. 'What did you do? Bribe Carlos?'

'As if I would!' Tom's blue eyes twinkled. 'No, I was more astute than that. I sort of got him talking about you, after you'd gone up to your room to take that call.'

Joanna sighed. 'Carlos has a big mouth!'

'And don't I love it?' countered Tom teasingly, causing a gurgle of laughter to escape her lips. 'My, did I say something right for a change! That's the first time I've heard you laugh, do you know that? You should do it more often. It suits you.'

'Thank you.' Joanna gave him a rueful look.

'It's the truth.' Tom was sincere. 'You know you shouldn't waste the afternoon in your room. That tan you're getting is really something.' He paused, and then asked: 'Have you been out to the reef yet?'

'The reef?'

Joanna was perplexed, and Tom explained. 'The coral reef,' he said. 'It's just off the eastern side of the island. Don't tell me you haven't seen the advertisements. It's one of the island's main attractions. You know the sort of thing—you hire a glass-bottomed boat and go out and see the fish swimming about in their natural habitat. You can snorkel, if you'd rather, or if you're really adventurous, they hire diving equipment, complete with a guy to give you tuition.'

'Oh!' Joanna nodded. 'Well, no. No, I haven't been there. I'm afraid I haven't done much sightseeing at all.'

'You mean you've been hanging round the hotel, waiting for this guy to call,' said Tom wryly. 'Hell, come on, Jo. What d'you say? Spend the afternoon with me, and I promise you won't regret it.'

'I'm sorry.' Joanna had to refuse him. 'I'm very grateful, honestly, but——'

'But—get lost, is that it?'

Joanna bent her head. 'Maybe some other time,' she murmured unhappily. 'Don't you have friends? I thought you were with some other young people.'

'*Young people!* What the hell!' Tom swore angrily. 'How old are you, for God's sake? Eighteen? Nineteen? Don't tell me, I can guess. It's this old guy you hang about with, isn't it. You've gotten used to mixing with his age group. I guess he's convinced you that compared to his millions, youth isn't important. Well, don't you believe it!'

Joanna gasped. 'It's not like that——'

'No?' Tom was sceptical. 'So what is he? Married or something?'

'It's nothing to do with you.'

'Okay, okay.' Tom held up his hands, palms towards her. 'It's your life, I guess.' He paused before continuing; 'And in answer to your question, there are six of us here together. But we all do our own thing.'

'And they're already fixed up?' enquired Joanna tautly, but Tom shook his head.

'No. No, of course they're not. But hell, what d'you want me to tell you? I dig you, Joanna, I really do. And I'd like for us to be friends.'

Joanna took a deep breath. 'I don't know what to say.'

'Don't say anything. Just remember it.' Tom shrugged. 'See you around, okay?'

'Okay.'

Joanna watched him go with mixed feelings. Perhaps she was a fool for not accepting his invitation. After all, the idea of spending the afternoon in her room was not particularly appealing, and after her conversation with Evan, she could have done with some light relief. But it wasn't fair to involve Tom, not just to bolster her self-confidence. It was up to her to do what she was being paid for. If she wanted to have the money to make a career for herself, she had to be ruthless, even if it meant betraying every principle in her book.

She waited until the sun had lost its heat before leaving the hotel. Evenings in Florida were still very warm, and the thin cotton shirt and matching pants she was wearing clung to her slim body. She had washed her hair and it hung down her back almost to her waist, its only fastening a piece of black elastic to keep it in place. She wore little make-up, just some lip-gloss and a matching eye-shadow, that gave her long eyes a slightly oriental appearance.

Ignoring the attention her long-limbed elegance

attracted, Joanna covered the length of Coral Reef
Avenue in fifteen minutes. Then, stepping down
on to the beach, she started off along the
shoreline, abandoning her high-heeled sandals and
splashing through the shallows as before.

Now that she knew that this was a private stretch
of beach, she was uncomfortably apprehensive of
being accosted before she reached Matthew's
property. It would be just her luck to be turned
back by some pompous servant, who would get a
great deal of pleasure out of making her squirm.
But in the event, she reached the final breakwater
without incident, and scrambled over on to
Matthew's land with a feeling of accomplishment.
At least she was doing something, she thought,
squashing the small voice of conscience, and
peeling off her shirt and pants, she quickly buried
them in the sand.

No one appeared to observe her entry into the
water. As she swam out of her depth, she glanced
back over her shoulder, but the gate of Matthew's
property remained securely closed, and beyond
that everything was hidden.

The water was delightful, as usual, and she
kicked her legs lazily, feeling all the heat draining
from her body. She felt she could have stayed in
the water for hours, and it was almost an anti-
climax when the fast-sinking sun warned her that
it was time she was making her move. With a
feeling of apprehension she swam back to the
shallows, and finding her feet, paddled up on to
the beach.

Surprisingly now, she did feel chilled, and all of
a sudden her plans seemed rather too apt. She was
tempted to strip off the wet bikini and put on her
shirt and pants, regardless, but to do so would be

to admit defeat before she had even started, which did seem rather foolish. Nevertheless, she quivered as she ran across the sand to the gate, and she wished the slick rope of her hair did not carry quite so much water.

The gate was locked, as she had known it would be, and she searched eagerly for some method of attracting attention. But unlike the front of the house, the back offered no convenient bell-pull, and she was reduced to rattling the gate and calling Matthew's name.

After several minutes of this, when no evidence that her presence had been noted was forthcoming, a faint trace of anxiety began to stir inside her. What if she couldn't attract his attention? she thought uneasily; what if she had to rescue her clothes and make the long journey back to her hotel on foot? It was all very well walking the beach in daylight, but already dusk was falling, as she had planned it would, and it would be full dark before she had covered half the distance. Stories of muggings and murder filled her head. She was alone, and helpless. She didn't even have anyone waiting for her back at the hotel. If she disappeared, how long would it be before anyone noticed her absence? One day? Two? Her body could have been disposed of in a dozen different ways in that time, not least the obvious one of being dumped out in the gulf.

Panic lent urgency to her hands, and she rattled desperately at the gate, her knuckles stinging painfully as she hammered against the fence. For heaven's sake, she thought despairingly, surely someone could hear her! To her ears, the sound she was making was deafening.

A niche in the fence presented a foothold, and

abandoning her attack on the gate, Joanna hauled herself up against the tall posts. It was hardly an elegant position, but at least from this vantage point she was able to glimpse part of the garden, and as her eyes searched hopefully for some proof that the house was still occupied, she saw a movement over by a wooden trellis. It was difficult to distinguish who it was in the deepening twilight, but it was definitely a human figure, and Joanna's spirits rose.

'Help,' she called urgently, 'can you help me, please? I—you see, someone has stolen my clothes!'

At first the figure did not move, and for a heart-stopping moment Joanna wondered if she could have been mistaken. Perhaps it was a statue, she thought faintly. People sometimes had them in their gardens, and she had noticed several stone fountains sculpted in human form. Her conviction that it had moved could have been a trick of the light or simply wishful thinking.

Then, just when she was on the verge of giving up hope, the figure moved again, but not towards her. Instead, it seemed to melt into the shadows behind it, leaving her to reach her own conclusions as to its identity.

Tears pricked at Joanna's eyes. She couldn't believe it. Whoever it had been, whether Matthew or his housekeeper, surely they could not mean to leave her here, unaided. It was possible they had not recognised her in the poor light, but even so, whoever she was, she obviously needed their assistance. She felt her foot slipping and stumbled down from the fence on to the sand. It was no use; she would have to go back. Matthew evidently guarded his privacy more closely than she had

imagined. She would just have to think of some
other way of getting into the house.

She was trudging disconsolately across the sand
when she heard the gate opening, and swinging
round, she saw a shadowy figure coming after her.
It was Matthew. There was no mistaking his lean,
loose-limbed stride, and she halted, uncertainly,
imbued with the uneasy conviction that he was
angry.

'Joanna!' She wasn't wrong. His low attractive
voice was vibrant with emotion. 'What the hell are
you doing here? For heaven's sake, if you wanted
to speak to me, couldn't you have used the
telephone? I gave you my number, didn't I?'

Joanna wrapped her arms closely about herself.
She was suddenly intensely conscious of the
scarcity of protection afforded by the bikini, and
Matthew's dark shirt and pants accentuated her
state of undress.

'I—er—I was swimming, and—and someone
must have taken my clothes,' she explained,
looking up into his dark forbidding features. The
shadows that were all around them made hollows
beneath his cheekbones, and darkened the tawny
glitter of his eyes.

'Really?' he said sceptically, regarding her with
cold disbelief, and the excuse she had conceived
back in her hotel room seemed to lose all
credibility now it was voiced.

'Yes, really,' she averred, realising that in spite
of her misgivings, there was no going back. 'I
wondered if I might trouble your—your housekeeper for a pair of slacks or a dress to go back to
the hotel in. As—as you can see, I can hardly go
like this.'

'Where exactly were you swimming?' asked

Matthew, making no move to take her back to the house, and Joanna waved an airy hand.

'Just out there,' she said, without being too specific. 'I—er—I came for a walk, and it was such a warm evening, I decided to take a dip.'

'I see the thief didn't steal your spectacles,' observed Matthew harshly.

'No—well, I kept them on,' said Joanna, touching the stem of her glasses.

'Isn't that rather foolhardy? Aren't you afraid you might lose them?'

Joanna sighed. 'I have swum with them on before. I'm very short-sighted, you see, and without them——'

'—you might mistake the shoreline, I know,' inserted Matthew drily. 'Exactly what kind of a fool do you take me for, Joanna? You don't really expect me to believe this cock-and-bull story, do you?'

Joanna shivered. 'Why—why not?'

Matthew shook his head. 'Where did you leave your clothes?'

'I—I'm not sure.' Joanna hunched her shoulders. 'I—I wonder, do you have a towel I could borrow? I really am feeling awfully chilly.'

Matthew took a deep breath. 'Very well. You'd better come up to the house.' He gestured for her to accompany him back to the gate. 'But don't imagine I believe this little drama. I may be a lot older than you are, but I'm not senile!'

Joanna pressed her lips together. 'I never imagined you were.'

'No?' His lips twisted. 'Go ahead. Up the steps and to your left. You'll be able to see your way in the lights from the house.'

Joanna climbed the steps gingerly, half wishing she had not buried her sandals along with her clothes. The rock was sharp in places, and she winced and fell back a pace as one particularly cutting piece of stone pricked the ball of her foot. Matthew, coming behind, practically cannoned into her, and his hands came out automatically to grip her arms.

'What happened?' he demanded, releasing her at once, but not before she had experienced the muscled warmth of his body against hers. For a fleeting moment she felt the strength of his chest against her back, the disturbing maleness of his thighs against her legs, and knew an aching deprivation when he abruptly drew away.

'I—I must have stepped on a pebble,' she said unsteadily, lifting her leg to examine her foot. There was a small gash just below her toes, and she thought how typical it was that she should do something foolish yet again.

'Let me see that,' muttered Matthew, coming round in front of her, but Joanna shook her head as she lowered her foot.

'I—it's nothing much,' she protested, wishing he would just forget about it, but Matthew was squatting down in front of her, waiting for her to show him.

'It's bleeding,' he declared impatiently, getting to his feet again. 'I'll have to dress it. Coral can be poisonous, and most of the rock around here has a coral content.'

Joanna sighed. 'I'm sorry——'

'Yes, so am I,' he replied shortly. 'Wait,' he added, as she put her foot to the ground, 'I'll carry you the rest of the way.'

'Oh, no!' Joanna stepped back. 'You can't.'

'Why can't I?' His eyes narrowed suddenly. 'What's wrong? Don't you want me to touch you?'

'Don't I want——' Joanna broke off abruptly. 'Don't be ridiculous! Why shouldn't I want you to touch me?' Her lips parted in unknowing provocation. 'It's just that I—I'm too heavy.'

Matthew's expression was enigmatic, but stepping towards her, he swung her up into his arms. 'I guess I'll survive,' he remarked drily, and strode towards the lights of the house.

CHAPTER SIX

IT wasn't far, but Joanna was conscious of him every inch of the way. With his arm supporting her back and the other looped beneath her knees, she couldn't help being aware of his every movement, and her breathing came shallowly as she tried to control her disturbed feelings. Her arm was around his shoulders, resting lightly on the silky material of his shirt and once, when he shifted her to a more comfortable position, her hand brushed the taut column of his throat. He flinched then, and Joanna felt as if her fingers had burned his flesh, but apart from that one occasion, he gave no sign that her nearness had any effect on him. He seemed to be holding her with a distinct edge of detachment, and even the scented hollow between her breasts, exposed by the cut-away bra of the bikini, failed to distract his dogged aim for his objective.

Elena Massey was waiting for them at the door, and her eyes took on a knowing insolence when they saw Joanna. 'Well, well, Miss Holland,' she observed, stepping back to allow Matthew to carry his burden inside. 'What a pleasant surprise!'

'Isn't it,' put in Matthew sardonically, setting Joanna on her feet in what appeared to be a kind of conservatory. The floor here was tiled with squares of rose-red brick, and there was a predominance of plantlife, growing in pots and planters, their thick exotic foliage reaching greedily for the louvred roof. The scent of their blossoms was paramount, a strangely heady smell that caused Joanna to look about her rather doubtfully, wondering whether Evan secretly suspected Matthew of growing cannabis.

'Has Miss Holland had an accident?' enquired Elena, closing the mesh door behind them, and Matthew gave her a telling look.

'Miss Holland has had *two* accidents, actually,' he replied, with some irony. 'Apparently she went swimming and lost her clothes, and now she's cut her foot walking up from the beach.'

Elena's eyes widened. 'Miss Holland went swimming in her clothes?' she echoed faintly. 'But why would she——'

'I wish you'd both stop talking about me as if I wasn't here!' exclaimed Joanna tensely, feeling shivery again, now that the warmth of Matthew's body had been removed. 'I—do you have a towel, Mrs Massey? I really do feel rather cold.'

Matthew's mocking expression disappeared, and one of slightly irritated concern took its place. 'Bring her a bathrobe, will you, Elena?' he asked, observing the few specks of blood now discolouring the floor of the conservatory. 'We'll be in my office. I must do something about this cut.'

'If you say so,' remarked Elena offhandedly, walking towards a door that apparently led into the main body of the house, and with an exclamation of impatience Matthew swung Joanna up into his arms once more and started after her.

'You don't have to do this, you know,' protested Joanna unhappily, feeling distinctly unwanted now. 'If you could just lend me some clothes and call me a cab——'

'I will,' Matthew interrupted her shortly. 'When I've made certain there's no danger of infection.'

'Oh, but——' Joanna pressed closer to him as he carried her through the doorway into a narrow corridor at the back of the house. 'I don't want to be a nuisance——'

'Then why did you come here?' demanded Matthew grimly, his eyes glittering with suppressed anger as he turned his head to look at her. 'You knew you were trespassing on private property. What have I done to arouse your curiosity? Because that's the real reason you're here, isn't it? That, and some perverse desire to make me take notice of you!'

Joanna gasped. 'You flatter yourself!'

'Perhaps I do.' He stopped at a door and manoeuvred her weight so that he could turn the handle. 'But the fact remains, you chose to play a game to gain access to this house, and what else am I supposed to think when you come here half naked?'

'I'm wearing a bathing suit,' she exclaimed defensively, as he pushed open the door of the room with his foot and set her down abruptly on a polished wooden floor. 'I don't generally go swimming fully dressed—do you?'

'No,' he conceded flatly, pressing a switch and flooding the room with light. 'I don't *generally* use a swimsuit either.' And as her face suffused with colour, he added; 'Do you realise how reckless you were? If no one had heard your cries for help, you might well have got more than you bargained for.'

'I know that.' Joanna flexed her shoulders wearily, looking down at the floor. 'I could have been murdered——'

'You could have been *raped*!' Matthew overrode her harshly. 'Dear heavens! Can you imagine what your father would say if he could see you now?'

Joanna sniffed. 'Well, you certainly took your time in opening the gate,' she declared. 'I'd almost given up hope of you hearing me.'

'*I* didn't hear you,' retorted Matthew, gesturing towards a leather armchair. 'Sit down. I'll get the medication.'

He went through a door to one side of the room and Joanna had a fleeting glimpse of a white-tiled wall beyond. It reminded her of the wall of an operating theatre or a laboratory, and she frowned as she considered this development. Obviously, Matthew was doing some work here, why else would he need an office, and she looked about her speculatively, wishing she wasn't obliged to find out.

Taking the chair Matthew had indicated, grimacing as her still-damp legs clung to the leather, Joanna examined her surroundings. A square mahogany desk was set at one side of the room, with a metal filing cabinet close by. A typewriter resided on top of the filing cabinet, and a pile of used manuscript spilled from a wire tray. There were various files and papers on the desk, but Joanna did not have the temerity to get up to see what they were. Instead, she looked round at the walls, at the posters set at irregular intervals, and the curious chart on the wall above the desk.

The posters mainly concerned world health. They were the kind of thing she had seen in doctors' waiting rooms back home. Posters concerning the third world mostly, with references to dysentery and cholera, typhus and leprosy. There were posters depicting the suffering of small children, left to poverty and starvation, the bloated stomachs of malnutrition contrasting grotesquely with stick-like arms and legs.

She had turned her attention to the chart when Elena came back with a towelling bathrobe, and giving up the attempt to work out what D.D.S. was, Joanna met her gaze levelly.

'Thank you,' she said, taking the white robe from her and slipping her arms into the sleeves. 'Hmm, that feels better. I'm very grateful.'

Elena shrugged and walked back to the door, but once there, she lingered in the opening. 'Would you like me to go and look for your clothes?' she asked, her tone laced with contempt. 'I guess they're still down there on the beach, if I cared to look for them.'

Joanna controlled her colour with difficulty. 'Thank you, but that won't be necessary,' she declared, ignoring the woman's sarcasm. 'If you'd be kind enough to—to lend me a pair of trousers, or a skirt——'

'You're too skinny to wear any skirt or pants of mine,' retorted Elena arrogantly. 'I guess you're just going to have to go and find your own clothes, after all. Unless you want to go back to the hotel like that!'

The sound of the other door being opened brought this rather unpleasant exchange to an end, and Elena had disappeared before Matthew came into the room carrying some dressings and an enamel bowl.

'I'm sorry I took so long, but I had to boil the water,' he remarked, setting the steaming bowl on the floor at her feet and squatting down in front of her. 'I see Elena brought you a robe. I heard her speaking to you as I came back.'

'Did you?' Joanna was still smarting from Elena's insolence, and wrapping the robe closer about her bare legs, she shuffled rather uneasily on the chair.

'I—what are you going to do? You—you don't expect me to put my foot in the dish!'

'In near-boiling water? I think not.' Matthew's tone was dry as he separated the dressings he had brought and extracting a phial of antiseptic from his pocket allowed a few drops to fall into the bowl. 'What's the matter?' he added perceptively. 'What has Elena been saying? I gather from your expression, she doesn't believe your story either.'

Joanna shook her head. 'It doesn't matter,' she said tersely, flinching suddenly when his hands reached for her foot. His long tanned fingers were disturbingly gentle as they exposed the wound to his expert gaze, and her tongue appeared unknowingly as she watched his ministrations.

It didn't take him long to clean the gash, and although the water was painfully hot, Joanna did not complain. She was too conscious of his lean wrists emerging from the turned-back cuffs of his shirt, of the brown skin of his forearms, overlaid by a covering of sun-bleached hair, and the plain gold watch on its black leather strap.

Even so, she couldn't help thinking what a tragedy it was that he had apparently given up the practice of medicine. How could he, when he was obviously so good at it? When he had obviously loved it so much? If she was ever ill, she wished he could treat her, she thought, although the feelings he aroused in her when he suddenly put his hand around her ankle were hardly ethical.

'Put your foot to the floor,' he said, swiftly dispelling Joanna's belief that he was as aware of her as she was of him. 'See how it feels,' he directed, and she shifted forward on the chair so that the square plaster he had adhered to the ball of her foot touched the polished boards. 'Is it okay?' he asked, looking up at her, and Joanna nodded jerkily. But the truth was, she was hardly aware of her foot, only of his cat-like eyes gazing enquiringly into hers.

'Joanna,' he exclaimed, with sudden violence, getting abruptly to his feet. 'Don't look at me like that, for Pete's sake!' He expelled his breath harshly. 'What the hell do you think I am?'

'I don't know what you are, do I?' murmured Joanna unhappily, looking up at him now. 'Don't look so angry. I—I didn't do anything.'

'Like hell,' muttered Matthew, turning his back on her and running agitated fingers through the silvery slick of his hair. 'Come on, I'll get Elena to lend you a coat, and then I'll take you back to your hotel.'

'She might not want to do that,' said Joanna sulkily, giving in to a feeling of depression. 'She said none of her clothes would fit me.'

'Did she?' Matthew half turned to look at her. 'Well, I dare say she was right. But that doesn't mean you can't wear them.'

Joanna bent her head. 'Why do I have to go back straight away?' she demanded plaintively. 'Why can't I stay here and have dinner with you?'

'No——'

'Why not?' She got up from the chair and faced him. 'Please! Please, let me stay. Matt——'

'You don't know what you're asking,' he replied flatly. 'Joanna, I—it's better if we don't prolong this. Inviting you here—it was a mistake. I shouldn't have done it.'

Joanna gulped. 'I bored you that much?'

'I didn't say that.'

'But you just said you didn't want me to come.'

Matthew sighed, massaging the back of his neck

with a weary hand. 'It's not a question of what I want or don't want,' he declared heavily. 'I just think it would be better for you if you didn't come here any more.'

Joanna sniffed miserably. 'Better for you, you mean.'

'All right.' Matthew nodded his head tautly. 'If you want to put it like that, better for me, too.'

'Why?' Joanna gazed at him.

'You know why,' retorted Matthew grimly. 'Aside from everything else, I am old enough to be your father——'

Joanna caught her breath. 'Is that all?'

'It's enough.' Matthew was vehement. 'So——' He walked towards the door. 'Let's go, shall we? Before the hotel sends out a search party for you.'

'They won't do that,' mumbled Joanna disconsolately, pushing her hands into the pockets of her robe. 'No one knows where I am, and no one cares.' She trudged across the floor to where he was waiting, scarcely feeling the cut on her foot. 'You could keep me here for ever and no one would be any the wiser,' she added, looking up at him through tear-wet lashes. 'Doesn't that appeal to you at all?'

'Oh, Joanna, don't do this,' he said, between his teeth, turning his head away from her. But when she moved to go past him, his hand descended almost compulsively on her shoulder. With his thumb sliding beneath the loose neckline of the robe, he turned her towards him, and when she lifted her face questioningly to his, he lowered his mouth to hers.

Her spectacles got in the way and he pulled them off, dropping them carelessly on to the cabinet by the door as his lips brushed sensuously against hers. But as he felt her automatic response, the tenor of his breathing quickened, and holding her still with a handful of her wet hair, he probed the quivering sweetness of her lips. Almost without moving, it seemed, she was in his arms, and ignoring his involuntary withdrawal, she wound her arms around his neck.

For a few brief moments he allowed the embrace to continue, but when her mouth opened wide to his, he uttered a strangled oath and pressed her back from him. *'No!'* he groaned, closing his eyes and leaning back against the door frame. 'I must be out of my mind!'

'Why?'

Her husky protest caused him to open his eyes again, and with a gesture of impatience he pushed himself away from the wooden support. 'Let's go,' he said shortly, picking up her glasses and pushing them back on to her nose. 'We've got to find you something to wear.'

Joanna gazed at him helplessly. 'Let me stay for dinner, Matt. Please!'

'Don't start that again, Joanna.' He went through the door and waited for her to follow him. 'How's the foot?'

'It's all right.' Joanna's response was taut, but after assuring himself that she could walk, Matthew strode ahead. They passed the door that led into the conservatory, and a few yards further on, turned a corner into the corridor that brought them to the front hall.

'Elena!' Matthew's curt summons brought the housekeeper hurrying towards them from the opposite direction. 'Take—Miss Holland and find her a change of clothes. I don't care what it is—a coat, a dress, whatever. She can change in one of the bedrooms, right?'

'As you say,' averred Elena politely. She gave Joanna an appraising look. 'You had better come with me.'

Without looking at Matthew, Joanna followed the woman along the opposite corridor. The tiled floor was cool to her feet, but she was hardly aware of it. She was engulfed by an overwhelming sense of depression, and she paid little attention to where Elena was taking her. They seemed to turn a lot of corners and the number of doors they passed was bewildering, but Joanna was too wrapped up in her own thoughts to care one way or the other.

She was eventually shown into a pleasantly-furnished guest room, with a soft woollen carpet in shades of green and gold matching the embossed satin bedspread. Curtains of a similar design hung at the windows, and when they entered the room Elena switched on an air-conditioning system by the door to stir the limpid air.

'Wait here,' she directed the girl shortly, and closing the door behind her she went away again, evidently in pursuit of the change of clothes Matthew had ordered.

Left to herself, Joanna sank down wearily on to the side of the bed. Now that she was alone, she realised how tired she felt. She was physically and emotionally exhausted, and she could not even summon the energy to think about what had happened between her and Matthew. She didn't want to think about it anyway. It was too painful, and putting her head on the mound of pillows, she curled her body up into a protective ball . . .

She thought she must have dozed, because she came to alert to the unexpected sound of an argument going on outside her door. She recognised Elena's voice. It was unmistakable, even though she was speaking in a language Joanna couldn't comprehend. But the heated male voice that was answering her was not Matthew's, and she sat up abruptly feeling completely disorientated.

Yet even as she got unsteadily to her feet, the voices ceased. The whole incident could not have lasted more than a few seconds, but that didn't make it any the less bewildering. Was there someone else staying at the villa? she wondered, and waited expectantly for Elena to open the door.

Elena did not open the door, however, and blinking, Joanna removed her glasses to wipe them on the hem of the bathrobe. What was going on? She wanted to go and see what was happening, but an uneasy feeling of apprehension held her back. It was nothing to do with her, after all, she told herself, ignoring the suspicion that Evan Price would think differently.

She frowned. It definitely hadn't sounded like Matthew's voice. She could almost swear it. And in any case, why would he be speaking to Elena in a foreign language?

She was puzzled, but as she turned away from the door, her eyes alighted on a pair of pants and a smock draped over the arm of a cane-backed chair. With a feeling of helplessness she moved towards them, convinced they had not been there when she came into the room, and then expelled her breath impatiently as the explanation occurred to her. Elena had come back; she had brought these clothes for her; and because she had been asleep, she had not wanted to disturb her.

Joanna shrugged away the uncharitable thought that such consideration was not typical of the Elena she knew, and hastily unfastened the cord of

the bathrobe. At least she had brought her
something decent to wear, and she would not have
to walk into the Hotel Conchas in her bikini.

The swimsuit had dried on her, but her hair was
still wet, and Joanna used the bathrobe to rub
some of the dampness out of it. Then, peeling off
the bra and briefs of the bikini, she used the robe
to towel her body, welcoming the sudden abrasion
against her sensitised skin.

The smock slid easily over her head, a couple of
sizes too large, but not noticeably so. It had a
round scooped neckline, elbow-length sleeves, and
a hem that reached the start of the tan at the top
of her legs. She was reaching for the cotton
trousers when the door opened without warning,
and when she turned to make her protest she
found Matthew staring helplessly at her.

'I'm sorry,' he muttered. 'I—Elena said you
were asleep—I was going to wake you—oh, what
the hell!'

He turned back to the door, but Joanna's voice
arrested him. 'It's all right,' she exclaimed, quickly
pushing her legs into the cotton pants. 'I—I'm
decent now, honestly. And—and I was asleep. But
I woke up.'

Matthew half turned to find her desperately
trying to keep the trousers in place. 'I'm sorry,' he
said again, more stiffly now. 'I should have
knocked.'

'It doesn't matter.' Joanna gave up trying to
use the belt as it should be used, and tied the
two ends in a knot. 'There. That looks all right,
doesn't it?'

Matthew sighed. 'It looks fine.' He glanced
round. 'What about shoes?'

'Oh, I don't need any shoes,' Joanna moved her

shoulders indifferently. 'I shan't be walking far, shall I?'

Matthew caught his lower lip between his teeth and regarded her steadily for a moment. Then he said harshly: 'Do you hate me now?'

Joanna avoided his eyes. 'Why should I hate you?'

'We both know.' Matthew jerked open the door and gestured for her to follow him. 'Come with me, I want to show you something.'

They went back through the house to the entrance hall, and subsequently along the corridor to the narrower passage that led to his office. Joanna, who had half expected him to take her to the car, knew a sudden uneasy premonition as they entered the quiet room, and she glanced quickly at Matthew as he closed the door behind them.

'Bring that chair to the desk,' he directed, and walked behind the square mahogany table to pull open one of the drawers of the filing cabinet. 'Take a look at these,' he said, spilling more than a dozen photographs from the file he had extracted, and Joanna, seating herself in the leather armchair, reached innocently for one of the black and white prints.

Nothing had prepared her for the ugliness of that photograph. She had been apprehensive when Matthew brought her back here, but she had not known why. She was not afraid of him, only of his anger turned against her, and when she first picked up the picture, she had been half afraid it would reveal some flaw in her own character. She didn't know exactly what she had expected—proof, perhaps, that he had discovered her real reason for coming to Mango Key. But the distorted image that gazed out at her from the photograph drove all thoughts of her own deceit out of her head.

It was the picture of an African, but the terrible scars that disfigured his features made any real identification impossible. His face seemed to have collapsed; there were no clear outlines, no definition to the bones, and the eyelids drooped above hollow eye sockets. Joanna was appalled. She had never seen anything quite so horrifying in her life, but she determinedly hid her feelings and reached for another of the glossy prints.

This time it was the picture of a child, a boy of perhaps ten or eleven, who was gazing into the camera. His was a face full of character, she thought, his thick lips curved back into a smile, but like the man, there were traces of the disfiguring thickening of the flesh around his nose, and already there were signs that his ear might be infected.

The third picture was that of a woman, dressed in traditional African costume, holding a naked child to her breast. After the other pictures, it was a relief to see that her features were not disfigured at all, and the baby in her arms seemed to be suffering from nothing more terrifying than hunger.

Joanna went on, picking up the photographs one after another, endeavouring to study them objectively. She was aware of Matthew standing at the other side of the desk watching her, and she wondered if he was waiting for some expected reaction. Perhaps he thought she would be revolted by the pictures of sick people, she reflected. Perhaps his intention had been to shock her. In part, he had succeeded, but she felt no sense of revulsion, only helplessness and pity.

When she had looked at all of them, when all the pain and despair in those ravaged faces had been acknowledged, she shuffled the photographs together and laid them on the desk. Then, knowing he was waiting for her reaction, she lifted her face to Matthew's, and met the enigmatic tautness of his gaze.

'Do you know what's wrong with them?' he demanded, picking the photographs up again and stuffing them back in the file.

Joanna moistened her lips. 'No, not really. Unless—unless it's leprosy.'

'What do you know about leprosy?'

'Very little.' Joanna was honest. 'I know there's no cure.'

'Do you?' Matthew's lips twisted. 'Well, it may interest you to know that since 1948 there has been a cure, or at least a drug with the capability of halting the disease's progress.'

Joanna's eyes widened. 'I didn't know that.'

'Not many people do.' Matthew's tone was bitter. 'To most people, it's still the source of fear and superstition it's always been.'

'But I thought——' Joanna broke off uncertainly, 'I mean—I suppose it's the fact that it's very infectious that scares most people. Like—like smallpox and—and——' she glanced at the walls, 'and cholera!'

'Only lepromatous leprosy is infectious,' declared Matthew flatly. 'That's the kind that causes disfigurement. Tuberculoid leprosy is not at all infectious, and both types become harmless once they're being treated. Unfortunately at the moment, only the tuberculoid kind can be completely cured.'

Joanna frowned. 'Those people in the photographs—they had the lepro—lepro—whatever-it-is kind?'

'Lepromatous,' said Matthew levelly. 'And yes, most of them did. One or two didn't.'

'The woman with the baby,' said Joanna at once.

'That's right. Her kind of leprosy is curable, and it shouldn't leave her with any visible lasting scars.'

'Visible?'

'Joanna, leprosy is a disease no one wants to talk about. People who have it can be not only "lepers", in the literal sense of the word, but social pariahs, living on the fringes of society, afraid to speak of their fears, because of the stigma of being diagnosed as a sufferer.'

'But if it's curable——'

'Drugs cost money. And in many cases, the disease goes undiagnosed for years because the patients who have it live so far from any medical treatment.'

Joanna hesitated. 'Why are you telling me all this?'

'I don't know.' Matthew thrust the file back into the cabinet. 'Perhaps I just wanted to frighten you.'

'Because that's what you're doing?' she exclaimed eagerly. 'Experimenting with the disease?'

'Partly.' Matthew flung himself into the chair opposite. 'There is no antidote, you see. No convenient vaccine to guard against accidental exposure.'

'You mean—your work is dangerous?'

'If you want to put it that way.'

Joanna caught her breath. 'But, Matt——'

'That's why it's better if you don't come here again. Don't run away with the idea that leprosy is just a tropical disease. It's not. It occurs anywhere where conditions help it to survive. These days it's mostly found in Asia and Africa, and the countries of Central and South America, because that's

where people are living in undernourished,
overcrowded conditions, with poor housing and
even poorer sanitation, but no country is immune.'

'Oh, Matt——'

'Listen to me, Joanna. This isn't easy for me,
believe me. 'I admit—what happened between us
earlier was as much my fault as yours, but it was a
mistake. It won't happen again, I'll make sure of
that. I'm sorry if what I say sounds cruel, but
that's the way it has to be.'

'But, Matt—if leprosy is curable, why are you
behaving like this? If, as you say, diagnosis is the
most important thing, then what is there to fear?'

'Nothing! *Everything!*' Matthew thrust back his
chair so hard it slammed against the wall and got
to his feet. 'Joanna, don't you understand?
Leprosy is a living hell! No one—but no one—
should take the risk of getting it, not when there's
absolutely no reason why they should.'

She looked up at him. 'I'm not afraid.'

'Aren't you?' His lips twisted. 'Oh, Joanna, you
have no idea what you're talking about. Come
along, I'll take you back to your hotel.'

Joanna stood up also. 'I want to see you again,
Matt.'

'No.'

'Why not?'

'I thought I'd explained all that.'

Joanna sighed. 'I don't care about your work.'

'I do.'

'Matt——'

'Oh, for heaven's sake, do I have to spell it out
for you?' he snarled angrily. 'I don't want to see
you again, Joanna. You're a nice girl, but that's all
you are to me. *A nice girl!* It's no big deal. Just put
it down to experience!'

CHAPTER SEVEN

DURING the following week, Joanna did what she could to put all thoughts of Matthew Wilder out of her mind. Instead of moping about in her hotel room, as she had been tempted to do, she forced herself to act naturally and joined in the activities that were regularly organised for tourists. She visited the marine centre and the museum, she paid for a boat trip and toured the yachts moored in the harbour, and she drove to Key West, and spent the day visiting Ernest Hemingway's house, viewing the famous paintings of John Audubon, and shopping among the craft shops along Duval Street. She told herself she needed this time to decide exactly what she was going to do now that Matthew had severed their relationship, but truthfully she was dreading her eventual return to England.

Two days after her second visit to Matthew's villa, her own shirt, slacks and sandals were returned to her. She wondered, as she opened the parcel with trembling fingers, who had found them buried in the sand. She suspected it had been Elena, eager to erase any trace of her occupation from the beach, and the fact that they had been neatly laundered seemed to confirm this supposition. She wondered if she should have had Elena's clothes laundered before returning them to her. It was too late now. She had had the concierge at the hotel mail the parcel the previous morning.

Towards the end of the week she telephoned

96

Evan. She had not wanted to phone him, but she knew if she didn't, he would begin to suspect her motives again, and sooner or later she had to try and convince him that her journey had achieved nothing.

However, with mixed feelings she learned that he was not in his office, and his secretary explained that he had contracted a virus infection. 'It's been so cold and damp,' she said, and Joanna thought how amazing it was that she should be basking in sunshine while England was still wrapped in the coils of winter. 'I don't know when he'll be back,' the secretary continued, 'but he said if you rang to tell you, he'll be in touch just as soon as he feels better.'

'Oh—oh, I see,' murmured Joanna, feeling an unexpected sense of anti-climax. She had been mentally gathering her resources for this conversation, and now she was going to have to wait to deliver her decision. 'Well, give him my best wishes, won't you?'

'I will.' The secretary accepted the polite rejoinder without further comment, and Joanna replaced the receiver wondering what she was going to do now.

She knew she should make immediate arrangements to return to London. She would be a fool to take advantage of Evan's illness to hang on here until he was better, particularly as she had few illusions that he would agree to pay her expenses now. She had not achieved his objectives, and what little information she had learned, she could never betray. She had to face the unpleasant fact that her days of beachcombing were over, and the prospect of finding a job back in England was all she had to look forward to.

Nevertheless, she put off making her arrangements to leave until the following morning. One
day more or less was not going to make that much
difference to her, and gathering up her book and
handbag, she left her room and went down to the
sun-deck.

It was possible to forget almost everything with
the sun beating down on her closed eyelids.
Stretched out on one of the hotel's sun-beds, her
striped blue and white bikini exposing most of her
slender young body to its glare, she let the
powerful rays numb her senses, and welcomed the
pleasant state of lethargy that enveloped her.

'Don't you know it's dangerous to sleep in the
sun?' enquired a male voice somewhere near her
ear, and Joanna opened her eyes reluctantly to
find Tom Connolly squatting down beside her.
Like her, he was dressed in the minimum amount
of clothing, and his white swimming trunks
accentuated the attractive tan he had acquired.

'I wasn't asleep,' she declared, propping herself
up on her elbows and reaching for her spectacles.

'Almost,' averred Tom, picking up the spectacles
for her, but holding them annoyingly out of reach.
'Hey, do you have to wear these? You look
stunning with them on, but you look even better
with them off.'

Joanna sighed, holding out her hand. 'If you
don't want me to fall over when I stand up, you'd
better give them to me,' she replied. 'What time is
it anyway? It must be nearly lunch.'

'It is. It's after noon,' agreed Tom, examining
the spectacles. 'What are you? Shortsighted, or
something?'

Joanna was too hot to get angry. 'Yes, I'm
shortsighted,' she said, waiting for him to grow

tired of his teasing, but Tom's eyes only twinkled as he met her impatient gaze.

'Then I guess you can see me, can't you?' he asked. 'And that's all that matters right now.' He lowered his tone. 'It's good to know you don't need them when you make love.'

Joanna swung her feet to the ground, searching for her sandals. The paved sun-deck was too hot to walk across barefooted, and after accomplishing this objective she cupped her chin on her hands.

'Are you going to give me them back, or do I have to call the manager?' she asked mildly. 'You've had your little game. Now I'd like to go and get dressed.'

Tom shrugged, looked at the glasses once more, and then handed them over. 'If you insist,' he said, straightening to his feet. 'But how about having lunch with me? I know a place in town where they serve the most fantastic seafood!'

'You never give up, do you?' remarked Joanna, standing up and wrapping a skirt about her slim hips. 'However, I've got packing to do. I'm leaving tomorrow.'

'You are?' Tom looked crestfallen. 'Do you have to?'

'I have to,' agreed Joanna, unable to deny the sigh that escaped her. 'I'm sorry, too. This is a beautiful place.'

She turned towards the hotel, but Tom put a hand on her arm. 'Look,' he said, 'if you're leaving tomorrow, where's the harm in having lunch with me today? Your old man hasn't turned up, has he? At least let me buy you a drink.'

Joanna hesitated. She was tempted, not least because she was dreading these last few hours, knowing that once she left Mango Key she was unlikely to see Matthew again. Spending part of the day with Tom might help to ease the situation, and she could hardly be accused of using him when he had been so persistent.

'All right,' she said, causing a look of delight to replace his previous diffidence. 'But I must change these clothes first. I'll meet you in the foyer in— half an hour?'

'Great,' he agreed, hardly able to contain his exuberance. 'Make it twenty minutes. You look okay to me.'

It was quite a relief to go out with Tom. There were no undercurrents in their relationship, no hidden motives beneath their conversation, and no sense of guilt for Joanna in accepting his hospitality. She was able to relax, and over a delicious meal of fried prawns and fresh crayfish, Tom told her a little about his background.

'My folks live in Newport,' he explained, tasting the Californian wine he had ordered to accompany the meal. 'My father's a lawyer, and my mother owns a couple of racehorses. She's very keen on horseflesh. She comes from Virginia, you see.' As if this was explanation enough.

'And what do you do?' asked Joanna, forking a juicy pink prawn into her mouth. Then she smiled, and added: 'Don't tell me, I can guess—you're training to be a lawyer, too!'

'It's what my father would like,' admitted Tom ruefully. 'But I don't know. The idea of spending two-thirds of my life in some dusty courtroom doesn't have much appeal right now.'

Joanna shrugged. 'What does appeal?'

'Staying here,' said Tom at once. 'Building myself a cabin. Spending my time fishing—and painting.'

'You paint?' Joanna arched her brows. 'I wanted to paint, too.'

'Wanted?' Tom gave her a quizzical look. 'Why only *wanted*? You've got plenty of time.' He paused. 'Don't you?'

Joanna sighed. 'I suppose so.' She didn't want to think about her own personal problems just now. 'So what are you doing at the moment?'

Tom grimaced. 'Going to law school. Don't laugh—I've just not made any firm decisions about my future yet.'

Joanna shook her head. 'I know the feeling.'

'So how about you?' Tom ventured. 'I guess you don't want to talk about this guy who's let you down, but hell, he can't have meant that much to you, can he?'

Joanna lifted her glass. 'Let's not talk about me,' she shrugged, hiding behind the pale liquid. 'This wine is pleasant, isn't it? I don't believe I've had Californian wine before.'

Taking the rebuff with goodnatured tolerance, Tom obediently started to talk about wine. It turned out he knew the wines of his own country quite well, and was interested when Joanna was able to tell him the vintages her father had favoured from France and Germany. The discussion took them through the remainder of the meal, and by the time coffee was served, Joanna felt relaxed and replete.

They strolled back to the hotel around three o'clock, and unwilling to let her go, Tom suggested they might have dinner together that evening. 'As it's your last evening,' he pleaded, when she started to refuse, and with a helpless sigh, she gave in.

'All right. But I do have to pack,' she said,

leaving him at the lifts. 'Thank you for lunch. I really did enjoy it.'

There were no messages in her room, but she had not really expected any. Carlos Almeira had seen her enter the hotel, and she felt sure he would have attracted her attention if anyone had called. In any case, who was likely to call? she asked herself. Not Evan, certainly, and no one else knew where she was. Except Matthew, of course, and he had made his feelings painfully clear.

She dressed for dinner without much enthusiasm, half regretting the impulse to accept Tom's invitation. Now that her last evening was here, the time was slipping away very fast, and an awful feeling of emptiness would not be dislodged. She knew that if there was any way she could stay on Mango Key she would do so, but short of applying for a work permit for a job she had yet to find, she simply couldn't afford the luxury.

Tom took her to dinner at a nearby hotel. It was a smaller establishment than the Hotel Conchas, but it offered a more personal service and the food was good.

'It's just as well I'm going home,' remarked Joanna, determinedly attacking the fillet steak he had ordered for her. 'I'm sure I've put on pounds since I came to Mango Key!'

'You can afford it,' remarked Tom, regarding her with admiring eyes. 'I don't think you have to worry about your weight. Let us poor males do that for you.'

Joanna smiled. 'You're very good for my ego.'

'And you're very bad for my blood pressure,' retorted Tom, leaning across the table to cover her hand with his. 'Jo, stay another few days. We've only just got to know one another. Let me show you what the Keys can really be like.'

'I'm sorry.' Joanna withdrew her hand firmly. 'I really do have to go home. It's a pity we haven't had more time together, but I'm sure you'll soon find someone else.'

'Now you're beginning to sound like that old guy you've been waiting for,' muttered Tom shortly, his good-looking face mirroring his impatience. 'Hell, Jo, I want to get to know you better. Once you go back to England, heaven knows when we'll see one another again.'

'Probably never,' agreed Joanna quietly. 'Oh, Tom, don't look so angry. You'll forget all about me when I've gone.'

'I won't.' Tom was adamant. 'You've got the wrong idea about me. I don't go around dating every pretty girl I see. I like you, Joanna, I really do. And I would like to see you again.'

'Well, that's impossible——'

'Why is it?' Tom leaned towards her again. 'England's not so far away. What part of England do you come from? London?'

'Perhaps.' Joanna didn't honestly know where she was going to live once she got back, but Tom took her reply as evasion.

'Come on,' he said, 'give me your address. Surely you can't object if I write to you.'

'I really don't know where I'll be living when I get back to England,' Joanna confessed reluctantly. 'Honestly, Tom, I don't have an address, not really. I—well, my father died recently and my stepmother and I don't—get on.'

'You mean she's thrown you out?' Tom was very blunt, but Joanna almost welcomed it.

'I suppose so,' she admitted. 'I—I'm afraid I upset her.'

'So you came out here to get away from it all?'

'More or less.' Joanna bent her head.

'And there's no old man?'

She hesitated. 'No.'

'Hey, that's terrific!' Tom was delighted, but seconds later, his enthusiasm faltered: 'So who was that guy who called you? I don't remember his name, but I sure as hell remember Carlos giving you the message!'

Joanna moistened her lips. 'He—he was a friend of my father's.'

'Is that right?' Tom sounded sceptical, and she couldn't really blame him.

'He was,' she insisted, unwilling to say too much. 'But if you don't believe me . . .'

Tom expelled his breath with a rush. 'I believe you,' he muttered. 'Okay, I believe you. If you say so.' He paused. 'So—I'll give you my address, right?'

It was a little after ten o'clock when they got back to their hotel and Tom suggested a nightcap in the bar as they entered the foyer. 'Just fifteen minutes,' he begged humorously, swinging the hand he had captured on their walk back to the hotel, so that he felt, as well as saw, Joanna's shocked reaction to the man who rose to his feet at their entrance. He had been seated on one of the low comfortable couches in the foyer, apparently waiting for their return, and at their appearance he left his seat and strolled towards them with pantherlike deliberation. In a black suit of fine-grained corded velvet and maroon silk shirt, he looked sophisticated and mature, and although he did not normally look his age. Joanna thought that tonight the lines that etched his mouth were infinitely more pronounced. She thought he looked angry with her, and certainly there was little sign of friendship in the hard line of his mouth. She felt sure he must have discovered why she was still here in Mango Key, and her eyes when she looked at Tom revealed her inner conflict.

'You were lying, weren't you?' Tom's muffled accusation was full of remorse. 'I guess this is the guy you've been waiting for.' He grimaced as he turned to leave her. 'I'd like to say you must be crazy, but I can see I'd just be wasting my time!'

'Oh, Tom——' Joanna gazed after him helplessly, realising that nothing she said could persuade him now, and besides, when she turned to meet Matthew's chilling stare, she knew that whatever happened, he was right. She had been waiting for Matthew all her life; only she very much doubted that Matthew had been waiting for her.

'Hello, Joanna.'

Matthew's curt greeting coincided with their meeting in the middle of the foyer, and she knew it had to be something important to bring him into the town and into the hotel. If only she hadn't accepted Tom's invitation, she thought frustratedly. Apart from the night she went to the house on Palmetto Drive, it was the only evening she hadn't eaten dinner in the hotel, and she wondered how long he had been waiting for her.

'Hello, Matthew,' she returned his words politely, glancing about her rather nervously. But no one else seemed to be paying them any attention, and releasing her breath unevenly, she added: 'Wh-what brings you here?'

'Who was that young man?' asked Matthew,

without answering her question, and Joanna sighed.

'Tom,' she answered. 'Tom Connolly. He's a guest at the hotel. We—er—we had dinner together.'

'Not in this hotel,' averred Matthew flatly, and Joanna shook her head.

'No, at—at the Flamingo Inn. It's just a few yards along the avenue. The food's very good——'

'I know where the Flamingo Inn is,' Matthew interrupted her heavily. 'So where has he gone now? Is he waiting for you? I shouldn't like to detain you if your—boy-friend is waiting.'

'He's not my boy-friend!' exclaimed Joanna uncomfortably. 'He's just someone I met at the hotel. I—well, I told him I was going home tomorrow, and he invited me to have dinner with him——'

'You told him you were going home tomorrow?' Once again Matthew overrode what she had been about to say. 'Is that true? Are you planning to leave in the morning?'

'I—yes.' Joanna had no real choice but to admit it. 'I thought I'd drive back to Miami and get a flight home the day after.'

Matthew took a deep breath. 'We can't talk here,' he declared abruptly. He looked down at her feet. 'Can you walk in those sandals? We could go down to the beach.'

'I can take them off,' replied Joanna promptly, her breath coming in rather shallow gulps, and Matthew inclined his head and walked towards the door, making it clear he expected her to go with him.

They circled the hotel, through gardens lush with palms and tropical vegetation. The grounds were floodlit at night, and it was easy to see where they were going. They passed the tennis courts and the swimming pool, then descended the sandy steps that led down on to the beach.

The low thunder of the ocean was a reassuring sound as they left the lights of the hotel behind and walked along the shoreline. Joanna was increasingly apprehensive of what Matthew had to say to her, and although she kept asking herself how he could have discovered her secret, the conviction that he had still perturbed her. Why else would he have come to the hotel?

'Why are you leaving?' Matthew asked at last, when Joanna's nerves were strung out like corks on a line, and she breathed unsteadily as she struggled to remain calm.

'I have been here two weeks,' she got out at last. 'I can't stay indefinitely.'

'I see.' Matthew pushed his hands into the pockets of his jacket as he strode beside her. 'And this young man—what did you say his name was?—he can't persuade you to stay any longer?'

'No.' Joanna was tense. 'And his name's Tom Connolly. He—he comes from Rhode Island.' She paused. 'I told you, I hardly know him.'

Matthew made no response to this, and Joanna sighed. She wished he would stop asking unnecessary questions and get to the point. There had to be a point, hadn't there? Why didn't he just tell her he had found out about Evan's commission?

'Tell me,' he said at last, 'if I hadn't been waiting when you got back, what would you have done?'

Joanna gasped. 'What would I have done? I don't know what you mean.'

'Oh, I think you do.' Matthew slowed his pace and presently came to a complete stop. 'It's your last night, as you said,' he added tautly. 'Doesn't it call for a little celebration?'

Joanna gazed up at him. His face was shadowy in the moonlight, but in the shifting shades of cloud it was possible now and then to glimpse his expression. 'What—what kind of a celebration did you mean?' she demanded unsteadily, and saw the sudden twist of his mouth.

'The usual kind,' he declared flatly. 'You're an intelligent girl, I know that. You're also highly imaginative—I know that, too. Don't tell me you can't interpret what kind of celebration I mean.'

Joanna caught her breath. 'I think I want to go back,' she said, turning away from him, but his fingers closing round the soft skin of her upper arm prevented her.

'What's the matter?' he demanded. 'Did I scrape a nerve? After the way you behaved the other evening, what am I supposed to think?'

'That was different,' exclaimed Joanna, trying to break away, but Matthew would not let her go.

'How was it different?' he persisted, his dark face grim with interrogation, and her indignation gave way to a need to defend herself.

'Because it was *you*!' she retorted, dropping her sandals to prise futilely at his fingers. 'For heaven's sake, Matt, what do you think I am?'

'I don't know what you are, do I?' he muttered, the expression in his eyes causing her to give up her puny efforts to free herself. 'How do I know how you react with every other man you meet?'

'Well, I don't go to bed with them, not *all* of them, at least,' Joanna retaliated, her eyes smarting. 'Oh, for goodness' sake, let go of me! I don't know what right you think you have to ask these questions! Just because—just because Daddy's dead, and you see yourself in some sort of *loco parentis*, you think you can come here and spy on me——'

'I did not come here to spy on you!' grated Matthew harshly, forcing her round to face him. 'And right now, I surely don't feel like your father! For heaven's sake, Joanna, what did you mean when you said, because it was *me*? What do I have to do with it?'

Joanna looked up into his tortured face, and suddenly her heart flipped a beat. 'Don't you know?' she asked, her voice low and emotive, and Matthew's free hand slid behind her neck, holding her face tilted to his. She had secured her hair at her nape this evening, the sophisticated style giving her face an unexpected maturity, but the urgent pressure of Matthew's fingers dislodged the silky coil, and it tumbled about her shoulders, thick and vibrant.

'Joanna——' he said hoarsely, fighting the urge to bury his face in that silken curtain. 'Joanna, we have to talk about this——'

'What is there to say?' she breathed, her hands reaching out towards him, encountering the fine fabric of his shirt and feeling the rigid muscles beneath. 'Oh, Matt, you want to touch me, I know you do. Why must we waste time talking about it?'

'Joanna——'

Almost against his volition, the hand that had been imprisoning her arm moved to her shoulder so that presently she was standing within the circle of his making. With eyes made dark by his emotions, he bent his head to stroke her lips with his, but Joanna was too aroused to permit such a gentle salutation. When his mouth firmed on the yielding sweetness of her mouth, her lips parted, and with a little moan of satisfaction, she pressed herself against him.

She knew he had not intended it to happen as it did, but even he was unable to control the flame of passion that leapt between them. Joanna's limbs melted against his, moulding to every hardening angle of his body, and she tore off her spectacles herself, dropping them beside her sandals on the sand.

'Joanna, this is crazy——' he muttered, but when the thin strap of the gown she was wearing slipped off one shoulder exposing the pointed curve of her breast, the groan he uttered was one of defeat. He could not prevent his hand from covering her breast with urgent possession, and the swelling pressure of the muscles between his legs made her irresistibly aware of what her body could do to his.

'This has got to stop,' he said raggedly, but Joanna's mouth silenced him, and the instinctive sensuality of her caress caused Matthew to lose what little control he had left. With his mouth still covering hers, he drew her down on to the sand, and the weight of his body on hers quickly drove all coherent thought out of her head.

'Your suit!' she protested, before the searching intimacy of his mouth made any other reality seem meaningless, but Matthew was shrugging off his jacket without any particular anxiety.

'To hell with the suit,' he muttered, his breathing laboured after the fervent ardency of the kisses they had just exchanged, and she lifted her arms obediently and drew his mouth back to hers.

She could feel every sinew of his body straining

towards her, from the taut strength of his stomach to the corded power of his legs entwined with hers. But it was the thrust of his manhood against her belly that made every bone in her body turn to water, and she had no thought at that moment of how inexperienced she was compared to him. She only knew this was what she wanted, what she had wanted from the first day she met him on the beach, and even the thin fabric of their clothing seemed an insurmountable barrier between them.

His mouth left hers to seek the hollow behind her ear, his teeth fastening painfully on her earlobe before moving on with fiery fervour to her bare shoulder and the creamy curve of her breast. The buttoned fastening of his shirt was rough against her softness, and he tugged the buttons apart to allow fine whorls of body hair to brush abrasively against her skin. But it was a sensuous abrasion, and Joanna's body arched instinctively.

It was only when his lips moved to her breast that she offered any objection to his sensual assault. No man had ever suckled at the burgeoning ripeness that surged uncontrollably towards his touch, but although her hands moved to thrust him away, the sight of the silvery fairness of his head cradled against her moved her to accommodate him. With a little involuntary cry, her fingers slid into his hair, her nails raking against his scalp as his eager mouth possessed her.

By the time his lips returned to hers, her body felt as if it was on fire, every nerve alight with longing. It didn't matter what he did to her, she thought, so long as he assuaged the aching need that was growing inside her, and her hands moved urgently down his spine to caress the thrusting pressure of his hips.

'We can't do this,' he gasped, with sudden vehemence, as if the intimate exploration of her hands had made him aware of the insanity of what was happening. 'Joanna——' He put his hands on the sand at either side of her and pushed himself up from her. 'Joanna, you can't have any notion of what you're doing.'

'Of course I know.' Joanna's hands stretched towards him, but with an abrupt, jack-knifing, movement Matthew evaded her touch. Breathing unevenly, he got to his feet, but she could tell from the way his hands shook as he struggled to restore his clothes to rights that he was far from being in control of his actions.

'All right, so you know,' he declared tensely, stooping to pick up his jacket. 'I was forgetting how emancipated girls are these days. But even I am not desperate enough to make love to you here on the beach, even if, for one of us at least, it wouldn't be the first time!'

'Stop it!' With a sob of indignation Joanna scrambled to her feet, pulling the straps of her gown back over her shoulders. 'Why are you saying these things?'

'To put the situation into perspective; to keep my sanity, I suppose,' muttered Matthew grimly. 'Joanna, you and I—it's no good! I shouldn't have come here. I shouldn't have contacted you. But dammit, I stayed away as long as I could. I hoped that you'd leave. But when I found out you were still here, only a few hundred yards from me, I knew I had to see you one more time——'

'Oh, Matt——'

'No! Listen to me!' When she would have moved close to him again, he kept her at bay, his fingers digging cruelly into her shoulders. 'I'm not the kind of man you should be having a relationship with.'

'Matt——'

'Hear me out!' His jaw was taut. 'You're young, Joanna. You've got the whole of your life in front of you! While I—I have already lived half my life——'

'Matt, please!' Joanna twisted helplessly in his grasp. 'Stop making judgments. Stop trying to rationalise something that can't be rationalised. You want me, I know you do—I can *see* you do. For Pete's sake, Matt, stop acting as if either of us had any choice!'

He let her go then, turning away to stare broodingly out across the ocean, and unable to bear the barriers he was trying to raise between them, Joanna covered the space between them. Sliding her arms about his waist, she pressed herself against him, and felt the involuntary shudder that ran through him at the yielding warmth of her body.

'I love you, Matt,' she breathed, putting her lips to his back, his damp skin tangible through the fine silk. 'Don't send me away, please!'

He stiffened then, and for a terrible moment she thought he was going to repulse her. But although he turned and put her away from him, his voice when he spoke was gentler than it had been before.

'Joanna,' he said, and the way he said her name was a caress, 'Joanna, what am I going to do with you?'

Joanna's tongue moistened her upper lip. 'Love me?' she suggested, hardly daring to answer him, and with a groan of submission he pulled her into his arms. But it was not like their previous embrace. This time Matthew just held her close to him, his face buried in the silken curtain of her hair, and she quivered a little anxiously as she waited for him to speak.

'There are things—things you don't know,' he said, at last, his voice muffled and indistinct. 'Things we have to talk about. We need to get to know one another, to give whatever there is between us time to develop. Don't you agree?'

He drew back from her then, looking into her face, and Joanna could only nod her acquiescence. Right now, the most important thing was to convince him of her sincerity, even if his confession had reminded her of confessions she would have to make, too.

'To begin with, you have to tell the hotel management that you won't be leaving, after all,' Matthew continued, and Joanna's lips parted in dismay when she considered what this would mean. She had already spent more money than she could possibly afford, and now that Evan was out of the picture, she had to reconsider her position.

'I—couldn't I stay with you?' she ventured, glad of the moonlight to hide her blushes as Matthew released her.

'Not now; not yet,' he said, picking up his jacket again and sliding his arms into the sleeves. 'It's better if you stay on at the hotel, Joanna. Believe me, I know what I'm talking about.'

Joanna bent her head. 'All right.'

But the tone of her voice got through to him, and lifting her chin, he looked into her face. 'What is it?' he asked. 'What's wrong?' He paused. 'Is it Connolly? Is he making the situation difficult? Because if he is——'

'It's nothing to do with Tom,' exclaimed Joanna

quickly. 'Really, it's nothing. I—I'd better be getting back. It is getting rather late.'

As she rose from picking up her spectacles, however, Matthew's mouth captured hers in a parting kiss, and all anxiety as to how she was going to pay her bill suddenly seemed unimportant. She could always pawn her camera, she thought faintly, before the hungry pressure of his lips set her senses spinning, but when her hands sought the thick growth of hair at his nape, he forced her to release him.

'I can only stand so much,' he said thickly, pushing her spectacles back on to her nose. 'I shan't sleep tonight, as it is. Don't make me lose what little self-respect I still retain.'

Joanna gave him a tremulous look as they walked back to the hotel. 'Will—will I see you tomorrow?'

'Do you doubt it?' Matthew smiled. 'I'll pick you up out front at ten a.m. Don't keep me waiting.'

'I won't.' They had reached the gardens, and before they reached the lights of the lobby, Joanna bestowed an impulsive kiss on his parted lips. 'I love you.'

'I hope you always will,' remarked Matthew enigmatically, his hand stroking her cheek. 'See you tomorrow. Sleep well.'

CHAPTER EIGHT

THE sea at that early hour was still cool, but Matthew welcomed its chilling embrace. He invariably swam before the strength of the sun had time to cast a warming finger over the pools along the shoreline, and in any case, the deeper waters of the bay seldom lost their sparkle. The water was always fresh and invigorating, and he usually found that it cleared his head in readiness for the day. But not today. Today was different. As he walked out of the dappled shallows to dry his lean body with the cream towel he had left lying on the sand, his thoughts were by no means untroubled, and the problems he was facing refused to be ironed out by a swim in the ocean.

Why had he done it? he asked himself for the umpteenth time. Why had he gone to the hotel? He had never done such a thing before. Why had he allowed the physical needs his body demanded to get the better of his common sense? For that was what had happened. There could be no other explanation. And the idea of getting involved with a girl young enough to be his daughter was positively ludicrous. Worse than that, it was pathetic, and the sooner he acknowledged that Elena was right, the sooner he could resume his normal existence.

Towelling his hips, he gazed darkly out across the luminous water. Everything looked different in the cold light of day, he brooded. Last night it had not seemed so improbable, so *impossible*; last

night, he had almost taken the irrevocable step
that put his relationship with Joanna beyond the
point of no return, yet this morning he found it
hard to believe he had allowed such a situation to
develop. He should have been able to control his
feelings, he should have been able to put all
thoughts of her out of his head. But instead he had
behaved like a lusting stallion, taking advantage of
her youth and inexperience, and arousing her to an
acute sense of her own sexuality. Her implication
that he would not be the first man to make love to
her had no relevance. Nothing could alter the fact
that he had almost used her, and if he had drawn
back before the ultimate invasion, his behaviour
was still unjustifiable.

Nevertheless, as he dropped the towel on to the
sand, Matthew was forced to admit that all the
rationalisation in the world could not explain the
need she had—*and still*—aroused in him. In
heaven's name, he flayed himself, what was he
going to do about her? He knew what he ought to
do. He knew what Elena expected him to do. He
knew the most sensible course would be to ring her
hotel and sever any future connection between
them. To continue with the affair could only cause
her pain, and he should know enough about pain
not to inflict it needlessly on someone else. But
what he ought to do and what he wanted to do were
two very different things, and he recognised his
own weakness when he put aside the thought of
telephoning the Hotel Conchas.

Pulling on cotton shorts to cover his nakedness,
Matthew gathered up the towel again and strode
grimly across the beach to his house. He had no
qualms that anyone else might have observed him.
The house next door was seldom occupied by its

owners, who lived in New York, and the elderly pair of Cuban retainers who stayed there rarely crossed the threshold. From Matthew's point of view, it was an ideal situation, and one which he had taken into account when he first bought the house.

Entering his gate now, he closed and locked it, before climbing the steps to the garden. The temperature was just beginning to rise and the roses that grew in great profusion beside the basin of a stone fountain were just starting to open their petals. Shades of white and cream and deepest crimson vied with the hanging shells of pale magnolias, their fragrance mingling with the delicate scent of purple and pink bougainvillea.

A man was working in the glass-walled conservatory of the house. He was busy watering the pots of orchids and camellias, pouring liquid fertiliser into troughs where the roots of vines that grew over bamboo trellises sought their survival. The air was misty with the spray from several sprinkler valves, adding to the humidity generated by so many tropical species.

However, in spite of his apparent absorption in his work, the man turned as Matthew entered the conservatory, his thick lips curving into a faintly conciliatory smile. 'Did you have a good swim?' he asked, his tone matching his expression, and Matthew looped the towel about his neck and lifted his shoulders in a careless shrug.

'I guess so,' he answered, pausing to cup an exotic blossom in his palm. 'Is this a hybrid? Or did you grow it from one of those cuttings Mendoza sent you?'

'It's a hybrid,' replied the man swiftly, and then: 'Matt, about Elena——'

'Not now, Henri,' Matthew interrupted him equally swiftly. 'I have to get dressed. I'm going out in a couple of hours, and I have some work to get through before then.'

'She didn't mean it, you know,' the man persisted, his accent similar to that of Elena's. 'She spoke—impulsively, recklessly. But she was only thinking of you, of your happiness——'

'I know that, Henri,' said Matthew flatly. 'Look, we'll talk about it later, right? I do have——'

'She is too young for you, you know, Matt. Even without——'

'Dammit, Henri, do you think I don't know that?' Matthew's temper flared. 'But I don't need either you or Elena to tell me what to do. I know what I have to do. Just don't—push me, that's all.'

Henri sighed, his scarred face full of compassion. 'Matt, I owe everything to you, you know that——'

'Henri, don't!'

'But I must.' The other man pressed his fist into the palm of his hand. 'You've been like a brother to me. Better than a brother, a father almost, someone I could turn to when everything went black——'

'Henri——'

'That's why I don't want you to do this. Why I don't want you to get hurt.'

'Me get hurt?' Matthew's snort of impatience was scathing. 'For God's sake, Henri, *I'm* not in any danger! I thought you understood that. Elena understands it.'

'Does she?' Henri drew a deep breath. 'I know my wife, Matt. She believes what she wants to believe. And that isn't always how it is.'

Matthew shook his head. 'You're imagining things, Henri. Elena is totally objective.' He walked towards the door that led into the main building. 'And now I must go. I'll see you at breakfast.'

But when Matthew entered the dining room later he found only Elena seated at the table, chewing absently at a slice of toast, gazing out unseeingly over the sun-strewn patio. She didn't get up at his entrance, though her eyes monitored his appearance; she merely indicated the fresh pot of coffee simmering over a low flame, and Matthew helped himself before taking the chair opposite.

'D'you want some eggs?' she queried, indicating the silver-topped warming dish, but Matthew shook his head.

'Toast and coffee will do fine,' he answered, taking a piece of toast from the rack. 'And before I forget, I won't be in to lunch.'

Elena's dark eyes smouldered. 'You're meeting that girl!' It was an accusation. 'You're a fool!'

'Maybe so.' Matthew spooned sugar into his coffee. 'Did the paper arrive?'

'Have you forgotten who she is?'

'How could I?' Matthew spread butter on his toast. 'Pass the marmalade, will you?'

'Do you intend to tell her?'

'Oh, I think she knows who she is, Elena,' remarked Matthew dryly, and the woman opposite sucked in her breath.

'You are deliberately misunderstanding me!' she exclaimed. 'Last night——'

'Did you know,' said Matthew, overriding her, 'did you know that the human body doesn't need refined sugar at all?' He paused. 'It's one of the things we should get enough of in its natural form. Fruit, vegetables; and alcohol, of course, only that's not to be recommended as a substitute. If we eat enough of the right foods, we don't need to artificially sweeten our tea and coffee and cornflakes.'

'So?' Elena was impatient. 'You're changing the subject.'

'No, I'm not.' Matthew swallowed a mouthful of his coffee and regarded her over the rim of his cup. 'I'm just proving to you that we don't always do the things that are best for us.'

'Oh——!'

Elena sounded frustrated, and Matthew bit into his toast. 'It's a well-known fact,' he enunciated, licking the marmalade from his lips, 'human beings are fallible. I'm only human, Elena.'

Elena clicked her tongue and then, abruptly, she pushed back her chair and got to her feet. After a momentary hesitation she circled the table to where he was sitting, and before he could anticipate what she was about to do, she went behind his chair, slipping her arms down and around his neck.

'Oh, Matt!' she breathed, resting her cheek on the top of his head.

His rejection was swift and forceful, sending her back on her heels. 'Don't do that!' he snapped, his own chair rocking after his sudden vacation. 'I thought you'd got over this stupidity! For pity's sake, Elena, your husband is a sick man! Don't you have any compassion for his feelings?'

'Henri stopped feeling years ago,' she declared bitterly, putting a protective hand to her throat. 'And you weren't always so fastidious, Matt!'

Matthew's jaw clenched. 'I was drunk——'

'And that absolves you?'

'Damn you, no! You know it doesn't. But it was only one moment of weakness. I told you it would never happen again.'

'And Joanna Holland?'

'What about her?'

'How much do you intend to tell her about your—er—research?'

'As little as is necessary,' retorted Matthew bleakly. 'Forget about Joanna. She doesn't concern you.'

'So you're not about to commit yourself to a permanent relationship?'

Matthew moved to the table and swallowed the remains of the coffee in his cup. Leaving the rest of his toast, he straightened, looking Elena squarely in the face. 'Like I said, forget about Joanna,' he ordered. 'I'll deal with it in my own way.' He paused. 'See you at dinner.'

The sleek grey Mustang drove smoothly out of the garage. Its use since Joanna came to the island had improved its performance, and he reflected ruefully how infrequently he had driven it before her arrival. Perhaps in that respect he was overdue for a change. Perhaps it was time he stopped living the life of a hermit. There was no earthly reason why he should continue to hide himself away here. No one knew who he was.

He grimaced. In truth, it had never been necessary for him to cut himself off from his colleagues in England, from all the men and women with whom he used to work. Three years ago it had seemed important that he should, but he saw, with hindsight, that pride had played the major role in that hasty withdrawal. Yet, at the time, it had seemed the only thing left to him, a bolthole into which he could crawl, to lick his wounds and restore his confidence. Here on the Keys, he had found such a place, and in the beginning he had never believed he would ever want to leave. He had companionship, he had his work; what more could he ask?

Nevertheless, it had taken some time to get used to the isolation. Matthew was not, by nature, a particularly gregarious man, but he had enjoyed the company of a close circle of friends and professional acquaintances, whose opinion he had valued. Without their approval and support, it had proved very hard to start again, but eventually, after establishing his laboratory and starting his own experiments, his enthusiasm had returned. It would not be true to say he had lost all interest in his previous existence. He still corresponded with one or two intimate friends, like Andrew Holland, whose work was not involved with drugs and vaccines and a disease whose numbers refused to decrease, but who could keep him in touch with the progress being made in his field. Andrew's death in the air crash had been a terrible loss, not just to him, but to the millions of readers who had enjoyed his work, but it was Joanna's appearance which had forced him to stop and take stock of his life. Now, as he drove to her hotel, Matthew wondered if his attraction towards Andrew's daughter stemmed from his admiration for the man himself. They had been good friends in the early days, long before Marcia came on the scene. Was it so unreasonable that now that Andrew was dead, he should feel a sense of responsibility for Andrew's daughter?

He sighed. It wasn't unreasonable at all. On the contrary, it was quite feasible, bearing in mind his knowledge of Marcia and her selfish, self-seeking nature. The trouble was, his feelings towards Joanna were not those of a friend or a father figure. They were feelings he had never thought he would ever feel again, and although, in part, she had encouraged the development of their relationship, he was older and wiser, and therefore to blame.

He saw Joanna as he turned into the hotel forecourt, and she saw him. Waving, she hurried across the stretch of turf that separated them, her long legs and lissom figure attracting the attention of every male eye as she strode over the grass. In beige shorts, made of some shiny satin material, and a matching vest, her limbs turning golden brown in the sun, she was totally enchanting, and Matthew's senses refused to respond to the tight rein he was putting on them. Unwillingly, he felt the ache of his own arousal, the close-fitting cotton pants he was wearing suddenly feeling too tight.

'Hello,' she greeted him breathily, evidently noticing nothing amiss in the taut, unsmiling face he presented to her. Without hesitation, she opened the door of the car and slipped in beside him, reaching across to kiss him before he could set the car in motion.

Matthew would have prevented it if he could, but the searching softness of her lips found his mouth unguarded, and before he knew what he was doing, he was responding to her caress. The unconscious sexuality of her mouth opening against his caught him unaware, and the sweetness of her lips had him hungering for more. His hands clenched on the steering wheel as he fought the urge to take her in his arms, but he wondered how long he was going to be able to keep his hands off her.

'Did you sleep well?' she asked, adjusting her spectacles, and he knew the craziest impulse to take them from her and make her totally dependent on him. Her lips tilted. 'I didn't.'

Matthew made a play of looking in the mirror, preparatory to moving off, and then, realising he had to say something, he replied: 'I slept very well, as it happens.' Which was completely untrue. 'I usually do.'

'Oh.' Joanna was evidently taken aback by his answer, but Matthew forced himself not to relent. Sooner or later he was bound to hurt her, and perhaps it would be easier if he could make her meet him halfway.

'Where are we going?' she asked now, as he swung round the cars parked in the driveway and negotiated the turn out into the road. 'I brought a skirt, just in case I needed one, but——' she glanced sideways at him, 'if we're going to your house, it won't be necessary, will it?'

'We're not going to my house,' said Matthew flatly, accelerating along the avenue that ran parallel with the ocean. 'I thought we'd have lunch at Bahia Mar. It's an island about ten miles from here. It's only tiny, you'd hardly notice it on the drive down, but it's a good place for us to talk.'

'All right.' Joanna accepted his arrangements without contradiction, and Matthew felt a heel. For God's sake, why couldn't he have taken her to the house? It might have been safer to talk there, within Elena's hearing, than at Bahia Mar, with its acres of dunes and lonely beaches.

'Joanna——'

'Matt——'

They both started to speak at once, and politely, Matthew insisted she continue with what she had been about to say. In truth, he was in no hurry to start a conversation from which there could be no drawing back, but when he saw Joanna's unexpectedly anxious face, he wondered if she had already guessed what he was going to say.

However, when she spoke, he knew he was mistaken. 'I—I was just going to tell you, I've booked my room for another week,' she ventured, but as she said the words, he sensed this was not what she had been interrupted in saying. For some reason she, like himself, had resisted her original intention, and he wondered what could be troubling her about their relationship. Perhaps she had had second thoughts, too, although the way she had kissed him when she got into the car seemed to negate this suggestion, he decided. Curiously, the suspicion that she might wish to extricate herself from the situation did not please him as it should, and anger with her and with himself caused his foot to press more heavily on the accelarator.

Bahia Mar was reached via the Overseas Highway, which Joanna had used to reach Mango Key. Now that she did not have to concentrate on her driving, she spent the journey taking in the delightful panorama of the bay, but Matthew found little to please him in the silver sweep of the bridges or the blue-green waters swelling beneath. He felt taut and impatient, and less than willing to examine the reasons for his ill-humour.

'What are those islands over there?' Joanna asked at last, apparently prepared to overlook his brooding taciturnity, and Matthew was forced to answer her.

'Just out-islands,' he declared, dismissing the dozens of bird sanctuaries and sand-bars that littered the ocean to the south-west. 'This whole area is one big national park, with countless deserted beaches and coves.'

'It's beautiful,' exclaimed Joanna, settling more comfortably in her seat. Her bare leg brushed his thigh. 'We should have brought a picnic.'

'We can get a hamburger in Bahia Mar,' said Matthew, shortly. 'That's the island, up ahead.'

A white dust road peeled off the highway down an avenue lined with palm and magnolia trees. To their right, a narrow lip of sand edged the ocean, and to their left, an inland marina was the harbour for dozens of small boats. There were sail-boats and cruisers, dinghies and motor yachts, and several tall-masted schooners, part of a flotilla of similar craft chartered by a travel company.

'Do you sail?' asked Joanna, turning in her seat to look back at the colourful scene, and Matthew shrugged.

'I used to. Years ago,' he conceded. 'Off the coast of East Africa.' He paused. 'When you were about five years old.'

Joanna turned back, catching her lower lip between her teeth. 'Oh, Matt,' she murmured ruefully, shaking her head. 'I thought we'd got over all that.'

'Over all what?' demanded Matthew ruthlessly, watching the play of emotion across her expressive face. 'Joanna, you might as well know, last night I said things I already regret. Put it down to the fact that I was jealous. Seeing you with Connolly really threw me, but I've come to my senses now. I like you. I like being with you. But anything else— well, I guess this is as far as I want to go.'

Joanna caught her breath. 'I don't believe you.'

'You're going to have to.'

She bent her head. 'Why didn't you just call me? Why bring me out like this?' She looked up, the silky weight of the hair she had piled on top of her head seeming too heavy for her slender neck. 'Why don't you tell me the truth?'

'Which is?' Matthew's voice was tight.

'That—that Elena Massey is your mistress, and she's the reason you can't take me to your house!'

Matthew's relief was so great he almost laughed. But instead he pulled the car off the road, into the shade of a clump of palmettos, and thrust open his door. 'Come on,' he said, 'I'll buy you some coffee.'

With some reluctance, Joanna joined him, and they walked up a grassy slope to where a small Spanish-styled square adjoined the marina. Canopied walkways gave access to a number of shops, many of which sold the kind of equipment needed by the yachtsmen. But there was a bar, and a small restaurant, as well as the outdoor café to where Matthew was headed.

Joanna seated herself on one of the white-painted stools, set beneath a circular parasol, and presently Matthew returned, carrying two glasses of black coffee and a carton of doughnuts. 'Help yourself,' he directed, straddling a stool and picking up one of the sugary confections, but Joanna just stared out across the sun-spotted water.

'It's hot, isn't it?' Matthew prompted, when her silence became pointed, and she shrugged her slim shoulders.

'I've got used to it,' she declared, her eyes opaque behind the lenses of her glasses. 'I think I'd like for you to take me back to the hotel.'

Matthew sighed. 'Joanna——'

'I mean it. I don't want to spend the day with you. I—I'd rather spend it checking out of the hotel. There's not much point in staying on now, is there?'

Matthew looked down into his coffee. 'Joanna, I don't want to hurt you——'

'You're making a damn good job of it!'

'—but surely it's better for us to be honest with one another?'

'Is that what you're being? Honest?' Joanna finished her coffee and got off her seat. 'Can we go?'

Matthew finished his second doughnut and swallowing the last of his coffee, picked up the carton. 'No reason to waste these,' he remarked, falling into step beside her, but Joanna didn't answer him, and he shook his head. 'Look, there's no reason why we should spoil today,' he exclaimed, as they walked down the slope to where the Mustang was parked. 'Let me show you the island, at least. Then, if you still want to go back, we'll go.'

Joanna hesitated, evidently torn by the desire to see something more of the area and the suspicion that he was using it for his own ends. 'Oh, all right,' she mumbled, pushing her thumbs into the back of her shorts, and Matthew felt relieved that she was not going to make a scene.

Leaving the car, they circled the marina, and then, jumping down on to the narrow strip of beach, they followed the curve of the shoreline. The sand was bleached white and scattered with shells and pebbles, and here and there a seabird could be seen, digging among the exposed roots of a sprawling mangrove. They came upon a group of campers who called a greeting to them, the smell of the food cooking over their campfire a delicious temptation to an empty stomach. 'I think I'd like a doughnut now,' Joanna said offhandedly, when the campsite had been left far behind, and shrugging his shoulders, Matthew handed her the carton.

While she examined the contents of the container, Matthew dropped down on to the sand, drawing up his knees and wrapping his arms around them. Following his example, Joanna did the same, and for a time there was a companionable silence as she munched the remaining goodies.

'Mmm, they were gorgeous!' she conceded at last, putting the box aside and wiping her hands on the tissue that had accompanied them. Watching her as she rested back on her elbows, Matthew realised that for the moment, at least, she had forgotten their disagreement, and for the present he, too, was unwilling to rekindle the hostility.

'You've got sugar on your lip—just there,' he declared, leaning towards her to point out the offending crystals, but the moment his eyes met hers he realised his mistake.

'Why don't you remove it?' she breathed, her fingernail probing sensuously inside the unbuttoned neckline of his shirt, and the quickening rise and fall of her breasts invited the touch of his hands.

'Joanna,' he muttered, fighting the shuddering urge he had to feel her naked body beneath him, but her teasing fingers were moving lower, and the blood was thundering in his head.

'Kiss me, Matt,' she pleaded, her free hand caressing the hair that grew at the nape of his neck, and his mouth moved to cover hers with uncontrollable passion. 'You see,' she whispered, moving closer to him, 'you want this as much as I do.'

Matthew bore her back on to the sand, tossing her spectacles aside as his hands roamed intimately over her body. She didn't stop him when he pushed the satin vest aside to expose her rounded breasts, or protest when his fingers found the buttoned fastening of her shorts and slid beneath. She was all pliant, all yielding, and Matthew's senses screamed for him to take her.

'Heavens, Joanna, we can't,' he muttered, but she was too bemused to let him go.

'Love me, Matt,' she breathed, 'you've got to love me!' and with a groan of submission he thrust off the rest of his clothes, and covered her body with his.

It was heaven to feel her warmth and softness beneath him, heaven to anticipate the pulsing sheath of her body surrounding him, but a trailing thread of sanity forced him to ask the question, and her response caused a shuddering spasm of self-denigration.

'Then we can't,' he grated harshly, rolling away from her to bury his face on his arm. 'For Pete's sake, Joanna, I'd never forgive myself.' He paused. 'I thought you'd done it. You let me believe you had.'

Joanna choked on a sob as she sat up. 'So?' she gulped. 'It's no big deal. Someone's got to do it. Are you afraid?'

'Afraid?' Matthew hauled himself up, keeping his back to her as he reached for his pants. 'Yes,' he muttered, 'I guess I am afraid. Afraid of despising myself more than I do already!'

'Oh—*stuff*!' Joanna sniffed miserably. 'You don't despise yourself for wanting to make love to me. You despise yourself for wanting me when you know Mrs Massey expects us to split up!'

Matthew swore as he turned to face her. 'For the last time, Elena Massey means nothing to me!' he declared savagely. 'For heaven's sake, the woman's married! And she's living with her husband!'

Joanna caught her breath. She looked disturbingly lovely sitting there, like a naiad, her hair a dark curtain about her shoulders, the tips of her breasts pointed and roseate. The flat line of her stomach drew his eyes to the line of tan at the top of her legs, and Matthew knew he was a fool to deny her. He wanted her so badly he could hardly think straight, but he couldn't take her virginity, not when he had nothing more to offer.

'But——' Joanna's tongue appeared to circle her lips uncertainly, 'Mrs Massey lives with you.'

'And her husband,' said Matthew heavily, reaching for his shirt. 'Henri Massey has been my research assistant for the past three years.'

Joanna blinked. 'You mean—he lives with you, too?'

'Yes.'

'I didn't meet him.' She paused. 'I did hear someone talking to Mrs Massey, though . . .'

'You did?' Matthew hid his sudden anxiety.

'Yes.' Joanna frowned. 'But how do I know he really is her husband?'

'Oh, Joanna!' Matthew spoke in a driven tone, and unable to look at her any longer without touching her, he got to his feet. 'Please—get dressed. Someone might come along at any minute.'

'Is that what you're afraid of?'

Joanna tilted her head to look up at him, and Matthew's necessity for deception was summarily abandoned. 'No,' he said, between his teeth, pushing his hands into the pockets of his pants. 'I'm afraid because I'm too old for you! I'm afraid because I have no right to be here with you! And I'm afraid of how you'll react when I tell you I'm treating Henri Massey for leprosy!'

CHAPTER NINE

JOANNA scrambled to her feet, grasping his arms when he would have turned away, and pulling Matthew fully to face her.

'Is that it?' she breathed, indifferent to her nudity. 'Is that what all this is about?' Her eyes widened disbelievingly as she gazed up at him. 'Matt, is this why you've been turning me off?'

Matthew drew an unsteady breath. 'Don't jump to conclusions, Joanna. I've told you how I feel. Henri —Henri's condition is just the crucifying factor.'

'You're crazy!' Her eyes were bright with tears of frustration. 'Matt, what kind of a human being do you think I am? Disease, illness, any kind of suffering—isn't it punishment enough, without adding insult to injury? What do you expect me to say? What do you expect me to do? You know I admire you for what you're doing. Dear heaven, Matt, isn't this just the kind of attitude you said you wanted to erase?'

'That's different.' Matthew bent his head. 'I don't want you involved with it, Joanna. I don't want to take any chance that you might——'

'But you said you could cure leprosy, or at least that you could halt its progress. This man—Henri Massey—surely he's cured?'

'Henri is responding to treatment,' said Matthew heavily. 'He's not cured. He's not infectious, but he'll never be cured.'

Joanna moistened her lips. 'But if he's your assistant——'

134

'Only for the past three years,' declared Matthew, avoiding looking at her, his hands clenching in his pockets. 'Before that, he was working with the World Health Organisation in West Africa. He's a South African by birth, but he's lived most of his life in black Africa. I guess he must have had the disease for—five, maybe six years, before it was diagnosed. He hid it, you see. As people will do, when they fear the consequences. Nobody wants to be called a leper, even today. In our enlightened society.' His lips twisted.

'But how did you find out?'

'It's a long story.' Matthew turned his head away. 'You don't want to hear it.'

'I do, I do.'

'Then for God's sake, put some clothes on,' muttered Matthew tensely. 'I'm not made of stone, you know. Just because I'm a doctor——'

'Oh, Matt!' Joanna hesitated only a moment, and then moved surely into the circle of his arms. 'Matt—darling, I love you, Do you honestly think anything you tell me can change that?'

'Joanna——' His use of her name was anguished. 'Joanna, have you any idea what your father would say if he could see you now?'

Joanna shrugged. 'Daddy's dead. We're alive. Isn't that what's important?'

'Oh, Joanna!' With a helpless shake of his head, Matthew reached for her, his hands sliding sensuously down, over her hips to the tops of her legs. 'Not here,' he breathed, circling her lips with his tongue. 'Not now——'

'I ache,' she whispered. 'Down here——'

'I ache, too,' he told her thickly.

'Then——'

'I've got to think,' he groaned.

'You're not going to send me away?'

'How can I?' he demanded, his breath warm against her temple. 'But I've got to be sure.'

Joanna's shoulders sagged. 'Aren't you sure?'

'Of what? Of my feelings for you?' he asked huskily. 'Joanna, when I left home this morning, I was determined to make you see how insane our relationship was.'

'And now?'

'Now?' He shook his head. 'When I'm with you, I almost believe——'

'—you love me?'

Matthew cupped her face in his hands. 'If only it were that easy!'

'It is.' Joanna twisted restlessly in his grasp, and then, when his hands fell to his sides, she turned to look at the ocean. 'Let's swim!' she exclaimed. 'Surely you can have no objection to that.'

'We don't have any gear.'

Joanna shrugged. 'You told me you didn't use any. Remember?'

'That was different. My beach is private.'

'Well, who's going to see us here? The place is deserted.'

'Joanna——'

'Oh, come on.' Her colour was hectic with suppressed emotion. 'Do something reckless for once in your life!'

Matthew hesitated, but leaving him, Joanna ran swiftly into the waves. She needed action, any kind of action, anything to drown the persistent anxiety that Matthew was not yet convinced. The water gave her some relief, and she swam out strongly, uncaring at that moment whether he followed her or not.

The warm body that brushed hers some minutes later caused her to open her eyes in sudden alarm. She had turned on to her back to float, closing her eyes against the glare of the sun, and the touch of wet skin against her thigh gave her a momentary start. The sight of Matthew's artificially-darkened head only a few yards away restored her confidence, however, and she took a few gulping breaths to slow her pulse rate.

'I thought you were a shark!' she exclaimed, as he swam nearer to her, and his mouth curved in amusement.

'I thought you might,' he conceded, revealing he had been teasing her, and she cast off her melancholy and gave a menacing cry.

'You—you——' She swam after him rapidly, diving beneath him when she was close enough, and grasping his legs to pull him down into the depths. But his response was to take her with him, and she came up gasping and spluttering for air.

'You shouldn't play games if you don't know the rules,' he taunted her laughingly, and she turned her back on him to put some distance between them.

This time he swam after her, but she was able to turn the tables on him by catching him unawares, and pressing his head down below the surface. Now, he needed to gulp for air, and she gurgled with laughter as she circled at a safe distance.

They played in the water for over half an hour, and by the time they swam back towards the shore, Joanna's limbs felt a little shaky. The solitary dips she had taken in the past couple of weeks had not prepared her for so much activity, and she stumbled as she tried to walk up out of the shallows.

Matthew was following her, and when she fell, he came down beside her on the shifting sand. 'Are you all right?' he asked, turning her over, and Joanna's mouth tilted tantalisingly as she reached up and put her arms around his neck.

'I am now,' she conceded, reaching up to touch his lips with hers. 'Hmm, you taste salty.'

'You do, too,' said Matthew, his eyes sobering as he took in her unconscious sensuality, and Joanna gave a little sigh.

'Do you want me to get up?' she breathed, running her fingers along the curve of his spine, and with a groan of surrender Matthew shook his head.

'I can't let you,' he said simply, lowering himself on to her, and Joanna's mouth opened to admit his searching invasion.

It was early in the evening when Matthew took her back to her hotel. The sun was already turning the sea to molten gold as they drove south across the wide expanse of ocean that separated the two islands, and Joanna snuggled close to Matthew as they reached the turn-off for Mango Key.

'It's been the most wonderful day of my life,' she murmured, turning her face into the hollow of his neck. 'I wish it didn't have to end.'

'There'll be other days,' said Matthew roughly, his hands tightening on the wheel.

'Will there?' Joanna tipped her head to look up at him.

Matthew's tawny eyes darkened. 'Unfortunately perhaps, there's going to have to be,' he muttered, his lips twisting.

'Unfortunately?'

'Yes, unfortunately, Joanna, have you really thought what this is going to mean?'

She did not draw away as she might have done earlier in the day. She was too aware of how easily their fragile relationship could shatter, and besides, she was beginning to understand how Matthew felt.

'I've thought about it,' she said now, her fingers closing possessively over his thigh. 'Have you?'

'I've thought of little else,' he groaned, covering her hand with his own. 'And even now——'

'It was good, though, wasn't it?' she breathed, her lips brushing his throat. 'I did—satisfy you.'

Matthew's lips parted with reluctant humour. 'Oh, Joanna! Yes! Yes, of course you satisfied me. But that doesn't alter the fact that I shouldn't have done it.'

'Oh, Matt!' Joanna heaved a sigh. 'If you hadn't made love to me, I think I'd have died of frustration——'

'There are other ways,' retorted Matthew unevenly, but Joanna only shook her head.

'It was you I wanted. I wanted to feel—oh, you know what I wanted to feel.' She coloured slightly. 'I had no idea it would be like that. Schoolgirl gossip is no substitute for actual experience.'

Matthew made a sound of impatience. 'Don't remind me!'

'Remind you of what?'

'That you're just out of the schoolroom.'

'I'm not. Matt, I'm almost twenty. I know what I want.'

'Which is?'

She flushed. 'You, of course.'

'You mean—marriage? The whole bit?'

'If you're willing. If not—whatever you say.'

'Joanna!' Matthew's voice was strangled. 'I know what my responsibilities are.'

Now she did draw back. 'Your responsibilities?' she echoed unsteadily. 'You don't have to feel responsible for me. I—I knew what I was doing, and if that's all you feel——'

'It's not all I feel,' snapped Matthew savagely, but after glancing at her pale features, he saw that she did not believe him. Uttering an oath, he pulled the car off the road, ignoring the objecting squeal of brakes and the protesting horns of other vehicles he was baulking, and hauled her into his arms. 'Joanna, you should know how I feel by now. I want you, I *need* you! I just don't feel I have the right to tie you down to a relationship you might live to regret!'

'Do you think I'll regret it?' she asked, combing her fingers through his hair, and he buried his face in her nape.

'Right now, I'm selfish enough not to want to probe that problem,' he admitted thickly. 'And if this wasn't a main highway, I'd prove it to you.'

Joanna's lips trembled. 'I want you,' she breathed wonderingly.

'Yes.' Matthew looked down at her, at the burgeoning fullness of her breasts swollen against the thin satin of her vest, and pressed her away from him. 'Well,' he added unsteadily, 'there's not much I can do about that here. But, later——'

'Later?' She gazed up at him expectantly.

'Hell, Joanna, don't look at me like that,' he groaned, turning back to the wheel. 'We'll talk about it later, over dinner. I guess you might as well come to the house.'

It was seven o'clock when they got back to the hotel, and Joanna gathered her belongings together reluctantly.

'Couldn't you wait for me?' she asked hopefully, and Matthew expelled his breath on a whistle.

'I think it would be better if I went home and came back,' he declared levelly. 'I—Elena's not expecting company for dinner.'

Joanna bent her head. 'Will she mind?'

'Probably.'

'She doesn't like me, does she?'

'She doesn't—approve of our relationship, no,' conceded Matthew flatly.

She glanced at him. 'She's jealous.'

'Joanna——'

'Oh, I'm not saying she has any reason to be. I accept what you say about her being married and—and everything. But I think she does have some—affection for you.'

'I think you're imagining things.'

She sighed. 'If you say so.' She reached for the catch of the door. 'What time will you be back?'

Matthew glanced at his watch. 'Eight-thirty?'

'Make it eight o'clock,' said Joanna huskily, and with a nod of acquiescence Matthew complied.

'Eight o'clock,' he agreed, making no move to detain her. 'Until then.'

Joanna's hesitation was scarcely noticeable, and she got obediently out of the car. But she watched the Mustang's tail-lights until other cars on Coral Reef Avenue obscured it from view before turning and walking into the hotel.

Carlos Almeira was at the desk, but she scarcely noticed him until he attracted her attention. She was not even aware that her vest and shorts were hardly suitable attire for the foyer of an hotel at that hour of the evening, until his speculative gaze awakened her awareness.

'Good evening, Miss Holland,' he drawled, his

dark eyes stripping her of what she was wearing. 'We've been paging you since five o'clock. You've got a visitor—from England.'

Joanna's stomach lurched with sickening dismay. A visitor from England! It could only be Evan Price, and her spirits slumped despairingly when she realised what Evan's appearance now could mean. Today had been such a wonderful day, a day out of time, that had proved beyond doubt that she and Matthew had a chance of happiness together. If Evan was here; if Evan, piqued when he learned of her refusal to help him, betrayed the reasons that had brought her to Mango Key to Matthew before she had time to tell him herself, any possibility of their relationship continuing would be doomed.

Carlos, evidently realising that something was amiss, regarded her with troubled eyes. 'You are not pleased?' he queried, leaning over the reception desk. 'You are not happy that your mother has come to join you?'

'My—*mother*!'

Joanna could only stare at him, and Carlos nodded his head vigorously. 'Your mother, Señora Holland—but of course. Who did you think your visitor was? Someone not to your liking, I fear. But relax, it is only the *madre* come to assure herself her little girl is not getting into any mischief, no?'

Joanna swallowed convulsively. 'My—Mrs Holland; where is she?'

'I was able to accommodate her in the room next door but one to yours,' declared Carlos suavely. 'Unfortunately, the rooms next door to yours were already occupied, but Señora Holland assured me it did not matter.'

'I'm sure,' returned Joanna cynically, still feeling rather sick. Why was Marcia here? Why had she come? Was she alone? And if not, where was the ubiquitous Mr Rogers?

'Shall I ring her and tell her you are on your way up?' asked Carlos, eager to please, but Joanna swiftly shook her head.

'That won't be necessary,' she assured him shortly, and then, so that he should not get the wrong impression, she added: 'I—er—I'll surprise her.'

'As she surprised you,' put in Carlos shrewdly, and Joanna gave him a tight smile as she turned away.

On her landing, however, she went straight to her own room, unwilling for the moment to face any kind of scene with Marcia. Somehow, she felt sure her stepmother's arrival boded nothing but ill, and she couldn't understand what could have brought the other woman to Florida. How had she known where to find her? She had left no forwarding address. The only solution was that Evan had had some hand in it, and that supposition sent her into the bathroom to drown her anxieties in the shower.

She was drying herself when someone knocked at her door, and still not prepared to face her stepmother, Joanna remained silent. But Marcia evidently knew she was back, and she called in sharp tones: 'Joanna! Joanna, I know you're in there. Open this door at once, or I shall be forced to call the hall porter!'

'What makes you think the hall porter will unlock the door?' retorted Joanna, pulling on a cream terry-towelling bathrobe and sliding her spectacles on to her nose.

'Either way, it will cause a certain amount of embarrassment, don't you think?' replied Marcia shrilly, and with a feeling of resignation, Joanna opened the door.

'Thank you.'

Marcia did not wait for an invitation. She walked arrogantly into the room, and Joanna was left with the equally unacceptable alternatives of leaving the door open and allowing anyone in the corridor to overhear their conversation, or closing it and permitting Marcia to stay. She chose the latter, primarily because she was only wearing the towelling bathrobe and she had no desire to dry her hair in full view of her neighbours.

'Well?' she said, closing the door and leaning against it. 'To what do I owe the honour of this visit? Don't tell me you were worried about me, because I simply won't believe it.'

Marcia shrugged. While Joanna was talking she had been looking around the apartment, peering into the bathroom and looking into closets, as if to make sure that Joanna was alone. When she was satisfied that there was no one else in occupation, she seated herself on the basketweave chair by the open balcony doors and crossed her silk-clad legs.

'You're right, of course,' she declared, surveying Joanna's bare feet with evident distaste. 'Concern for you was never my strong point. However, when Evan told me where you were and what you were doing, I decided the time had come for us to get better acquainted.'

'Better acquainted?' Joanna shook her head. 'I don't know what you mean.' Though her heart had plummeted at the mention of Evan's name. 'Where's your fiancé? Is it wise to leave him on the loose when you're all these miles away?'

'Howard? Oh!' Marcia dismissed her erstwhile fiancé with a careless movement of her hand. 'You were right about him, after all. He was only after your father's money. I should have guessed, but there we are. We all make mistakes. Howard's was that I found him out.'

Joanna moved away from the door. 'You mean, if you hadn't found him out, you'd have married him?' She was appalled. 'You have a strange morality.'

'Morality?' Marcia gave a little laugh. 'My dear girl, morality doesn't come into it. Howard was—*is*—a virile man. For a time, he gave me what I wanted. I thought that was enough, but it wasn't. And when I discovered he was sleeping with his secretary as well as me——' She shrugged. 'He might have waited until after the ceremony.'

Joanna reached for a towel and began rubbing her hair. 'What do you really want, Marcia?' she asked, the memory of the afternoon she had spent with Matthew being marred by these sordid revelations. She had looked forward to this time alone to think about him, to remember the touch of his hands on her body, the feel of him on her, and in her, bringing her body to a peak of excitement that had left her feeling drowsy and languid, and satiated with pleasure . . .

'Where have you been all afternoon?' Marcia demanded, without answering her question. 'I suppose you've been out with that young American the receptionist told me you were friendly with. What did he say his name was? Collins, Conlon——'

'I think you mean Tom Connolly,' said Joanna tightly, her thoughts racing. If Marcia believed she had been out with Tom, why should she undeceive her? She had dreaded having to confess her relationship with Matthew to Marcia. She needed to see Matthew first, to talk to him, to tell him the truth. Whatever reason had brought Marcia to Mango Key, she must not allow her to gain the advantage.

'All right.' Marcia was impatient. 'Connolly, then. Is that where you've been? Out with him?'

'We—we went to Bahia Mar,' said Joanna, without actually lying to her. 'It's an island, about ten miles back along the causeway. We went swimming.'

'Really?' Marcia didn't sound particularly interested. 'And Matt? You've seen Matt, haven't you? Evan told me that you had. How is he? What does he look like? What have you found out?'

'Wait a minute . . .' Joanna moistened her dry lips. 'What do you know about Matt—about Matthew Wilder? What did Evan tell you? How did you come to see him, anyway?'

Marcia sighed. 'Does it matter?'

'I think so.'

'Oh, very well.' Marcia shrugged. 'If you must know, people started asking questions.'

'About Matt—Matthew?' Joanna was horrified.

'No, of course not.' Happily, Marcia seemed not to have noticed her slip. 'About you, of course; about where you were, where you'd gone!'

Joanna took a steadying breath. 'And you couldn't tell them.'

'That's right.' Marcia was offhand. 'I told everyone I was sure you were all right—you know what young people are, that sort of thing—but I was being made to feel I'd—abandoned you.'

'You had.'

'Be that as it may, I felt obliged to discover your

whereabouts. Imagine my astonishment when I learned that you were out here in Florida, trying to contact Matt Wilder!'

Joanna's throat felt parched. 'You spoke to Evan.'

'Eventually,' Marcia nodded. 'Of course, he didn't want to tell me, but I persuaded him. I can be very persuasive.'

Joanna could feel a pulse beginning to hammer behind her temple. 'What made you contact Evan?'

'My dear, I'd contacted everyone else. I actually spoke to his wife first. Dear Cynthia! Evan's been ill, you know, he's had 'flu or something. In consequence, his secretary has been relaying messages from the office.'

'And Cynthia intercepted mine,' interjected Joanna flatly, and Marcia nodded.

'Apparently Evan was furious that Cynthia had told me. But it was too late then. I threatened him with a lawsuit if he didn't declare your whereabouts. You can imagine how he reacted to that.'

Joanna reached for her comb and began threading its teeth through her long hair. 'That still doesn't explain why you're here. Surely, if you knew where I was, that was sufficient to pacify your—friends.'

'Oh, yes,' Marcia nodded, examining her lacquered fingernails with a critical eye. 'As soon as I knew where you were, I spread it around that you were taking a holiday with some friends before coming back to take up that course at art college.'

Joanna stated at her. 'But you said——'

'I was hasty.' Marcia's cold blue eyes bored into hers. 'I've decided to support you, until you've got the qualifications to support yourself. It's the least I can do for Drew's daughter, isn't it? And naturally, I shall expect you to return to Ashworth Terrace.'

'More social pressure?' enquired Joanna cynically. 'Oh, Marcia, things have changed since I left.'

Marcia's nostrils flared. 'Don't bait me, Joanna. I can change my mind again, you know.'

'And risk the chance of social ostracism? I don't think so.' She made a helpless gesture. 'I didn't know anybody cared.'

Marcia got to her feet. 'Don't get sentimental, Joanna. You know I can't bear it. Just tell me when you expect to see Matt Wilder again, and I'll leave you to get dressed.'

Matt!

Joanna cast a surreptitious glance at her watch. She was wasting time. Matthew was coming to pick her up in less than half an hour, and she had to get rid of Marcia before then.

'Wh-why do you want to know?' she asked now, schooling her features. She still didn't know why Marcia had made the trip, and anxiety, like a snake, was uncoiling inside her.

'What?' Marcia turned from her contemplation of her reflection in the long mirror backing the bathroom door and shrugged delicately. 'Why do I want to know when you'll be seeing Matt again? Why, because I want to see him, of course. Matt and I are old—friends. Didn't he mention it?'

Joanna hesitated. 'He admitted he knew you.'

'Well, of course. He and Andrew were close friends.'

'I know.'

'Oh, yes, that's right. He used to come to the house when you were a little girl, didn't he? Before—before I married your father.'

Joanna nodded.

'Has he changed much? Does he look much older?' Marcia caught her breath. 'Oh, I don't suppose you'd remember. Grown-ups are grown-ups to a child.'

'I'm not a child now, Marcia.'

'I know that. That's why I'm asking you: how is he? Does he look well? I can't wait to see him. It's more than five years since I bumped into him in Oxford Street.'

'In Oxford Street?' Joanna frowned. 'But Daddy used to see him regularly. He never came to the house when I was home from school, but I assumed that while I was away——'

Marcia expelled her breath rather irritably, and then, as if realising she would have to explain, she said: 'Drew could hardly invite him to the house, could he? I mean—all right, we're civilised people, but I was the one bone of contention between them. After we were married, we never met socially. Drew made up with Matt, but Matt and I—well, I suppose it would have been too painful!'

Joanna put down her comb. 'What do you mean?' she exclaimed, the blood turning cold in her veins. 'Matt and you? I don't understand any of this.'

'Oh, Joanna!' Marcia was impatient. 'You were a child. You knew nothing about it. And now it's all in the past.'

'Marcia!'

'Well, if you must know, Matt and I were engaged when he introduced me to your father.'

'What!' Joanna could feel her whole body

shaking, but fortunately Marcia seemed unaware of it.

'It's true. I'd known Matt for a number of years. We grew up in the same neighbourhood in Staines. We went to the same school. But he was always interested in science even in those days. He passed some exam and went on to one of those state-assisted public schools and I believe he did very well.' She paused. 'Anyway, when I met him again, he was working at a hospital in Kenya. Oh, not when I met him—that was in London. He was home on holiday, visiting his father; his mother was dead. I was working for an estate agent in Windsor. It was a dead bore. I was restless, I needed a change of scene. The idea of going to live in Africa seemed to offer everything I wanted—freedom from work, a chance to travel and see something of the world; and an escape from the rigours of trying to make ends meet.'

Joanna shook her head unsteadily. 'And—and Matt?'

'Oh, yes.' Marcia adopted a knowing expression. 'And Matt, of course. No woman in her right mind would have overlooked Matt in those days.'

'Yet—yet you——'

'—gave him up?' Marcia grimaced. 'Yes, I did that, didn't I? I must have been crazy.'

'Crazy!'

'Yes, crazy.' Marcia made a frustrated sound. 'Oh, don't look at me like that. I know you idolised your father, and certainly I believed he could give me a better life. Materially, he had so much more to offer than Matt, and I was blinded by his success. But your father was not a passionate man, Joanna. I'm sorry if this offends your sensibilities, but it's true. He was much too—

gentle, too sensitive, too considerate of my feelings. Whereas Matt—Matt was all male——'

'Stop it!' Joanna put her hands over her ears. 'I don't want to hear any more. You—you're horrible! Disgusting! How can you talk like this to me, to—to his daughter!'

Marcia grimaced. 'Joanna, Drew is dead. What I say now can't hurt him. As for Matt——' she lifted her shoulders, 'I had no idea where he was until Evan Price told me what you were doing out here.' She uttered an excited little laugh. 'He should have asked me to do it. After all, it was I who gave him the diaries.'

Joanna couldn't look at her. She felt sick, and disorientated, unable to take in half of what Marcia was saying. All that seemed relevant at this moment was that Matthew had once been engaged to her stepmother, and he had not seen fit to apprise her of the fact. How could he? she thought, the throbbing in her head becoming worse. How could he have made love to her, without telling her of that previous relationship? Perhaps he had had no intention of telling her, ever. Perhaps he saw in their association a chance to get even with the woman who had walked out on him almost ten years ago. It was not so unreasonable. In spite of his assertion that he was too old for her, he had made love to her, not once, but twice, during that long, blissful afternoon. And Marcia must have hurt him. Why else would he have stayed away from Ashworth Terrace all these years? That was why she, Joanna, had not seen him since she was a child. Because of Marcia!

'So now you know,' declared her stepmother carelessly. 'Drew's death was not the tragedy to me it evidently was to you. Oh, I cared for him, I'm not denying it. He was sweet to me. But now I'm rich, and free, and I can't wait to see Matt again.'

Joanna had one last question to ask: 'But you're older than he is, aren't you?'

Marcia's lips thinned. 'Just a couple of years, that's all. What's a couple of years at my age? I think I've worn remarkably well, don't you? I doubt if anyone would take me for more than thirty-five.'

Joanna bent her head and made no reply. It was probably true, she thought dully. Marcia did not look her age. While she felt at least double hers.

'Well?' Marcia was growing restless again. 'Are you going to tell me about Matt, or has this affair you've been having with your young American friend blinded you to the fact that Evan's supposedly paying your way out here?'

'What?' Joanna forced herself to concentrate on what Marcia was saying. 'Oh, no. No.' She put unsteady fingers to her head, knowing she was going to have to make a decision. 'I—er—I'm supposed to be having dinner with him tonight.'

'Tonight? With Matt?' Marcia gazed at her disbelievingly. 'You mean you've let me go babbling on when all the time you knew that Matt was coming here?'

'In fifteen minutes,' agreed Joanna expressionlessly, and Marcia uttered a dismayed cry.

'Fifteen minutes?' she echoed. 'I'll never make it.' She swung around on her heels and made for the door. 'But I'll have to. Wait for me, Joanna. I insist you wait for me. I want to see Matt's face when he discovers I'm here.'

'No—that is—I shan't be coming,' said Joanna

heavily. 'As—as a matter of fact, I'd be glad if you'd go instead of me. I'm not feeling very well. I think I've had too much sun.'

'Oh, Joanna!' Marcia was irritable.

'Well!' Joanna was defensive. 'It's all right. You don't need me. You'll have plenty to talk about. And—and Matt will understand, when he sees you.'

'You could be right.' Marcia was evidently considering this development more favourably. 'Well, why not? Where are you meeting him, and at what time?'

'Eight o'clock. In the foyer,' answered Joanna tautly, putting the comb aside and getting to her feet. 'You'll recognise him. He doesn't have a beard any more.'

'He's clean-shaven?'

'Yes.'

Marcia nodded, her lips curving in evident anticipation. Watching the light of avidity appearing in her stepmother's eyes, Joanna felt her stomach contract and the taste of bile in her throat.

'You'll have to excuse me,' she choked, racing for the bathroom, and as she vomited into the basin, Marcia's parting comment rung in her ears.

'I hope you haven't done anything foolish, darling,' her stepmother called. 'It would be rather inconsiderate of you to get pregnant now!'

CHAPTER TEN

JOANNA didn't bother getting dressed. There didn't seem much point when she had no intention of leaving her room, and as she didn't feel hungry, she didn't order any food either. Instead she curled up on her bed in front of the television, hoping the bland diet of game shows would numb her mind to what was happening.

It was a false hope. Even the presence of an endless succession of contestants could not erase the pain of imagining Matthew and Marcia together, and her eyes were drawn continually towards the face of her watch as the pointers crept slowly from eight, to eight-fifteen, to eight-thirty. What were they doing? she wondered. How had Matthew reacted when Marcia appeared to meet him instead of her? Recalling the impatience in his voice when he had spoken of her stepmother, she suspected Marcia would not have it all her own way, but given time he must surely find it in his heart to forgive her. She wondered whether he would take Marcia back to his house. She wondered what Elena Massey would make of her. At least she had avoided what could have been an embarrassing confrontation, and if Matthew despised her for her cowardice, that was better than facing certain humiliation. He might even feel a trace of regret that their affair was over. They had been good together; her skin prickled in remembrance. But Marcia would make him forget. She was so much more experienced . . .

As the hands on her watch crawled to eight-forty-five, Joanna made a pillow for her head with her arms and curled up into a ball. It didn't seem possible that this time last evening she had been eating a farewell dinner with Tom at the Flamingo Inn. So much had happened since last night, so much that had turned her world upside-down. Perhaps it would have been better if she had left this morning, though, as she had planned. Then she would not have had to see Marcia; they would not have had that conversation; and she might never have learned of Marcia's relationship with the man with whom she had fallen so hopelessly in love.

She sighed, her thumb probing insistently at her lips. If she had left this morning, of course, she would not have had this day with Matthew either, this day, which had seemed so perfect until Marcia turned up. It had been such a beautiful day, a day out of time, she reflected bitterly, but perhaps a day to remember when everything else turned black. Just thinking about Matthew brought a feeling of lassitude to her limbs, and she ached with the realisation that she had probably destroyed any chance of their ever being together again. But he had never said he loved her. He had said he wanted her and needed her, but love was a word which seemed absent from his vocabulary. Why? Was it because of Marcia? Had he loved only once in his life, never to love again? The idea seemed to possess a painful kind of logic, and what chance did she have of keeping his affection, when the woman he really wanted was no longer out of reach?

A sudden hammering at her door brought her upright with a start. What time was it? she wondered, groping for her watch. Ten to nine! She swallowed convulsively. What had happened?

'Joanna! Joanna, are you in there?'

As before, it was Marcia's voice that demanded entry, and hardly stopping to think what she was doing, Joanna scrambled off the bed and went to answer it. Swinging open the door, she gazed bewilderedly at her stepmother as Marcia marched into the room, and then, realising with belated relief that she was alone, she closed the door behind her.

It was obvious that Marcia was in a temper. Her small face was suffused with colour, and the light of battle was still sparkling in her eyes. She paced angrily back and forth across the floor as Joanna waited for her to speak, and then swung round on her stepdaughter, as if she was to blame for everything.

'You little bitch!' she spat, her mouth working furiously. 'What have you been telling Matt about me? What lies have you been spreading about the way I've treated you? Just because we had an argument over Howard, who I'm sure you secretly fancied yourself, you've come out here and cast pitiful aspersions on my character! How dare you? How dare you? For two pins, I'd take you to court for slander!'

Joanna shook her head, trying to arouse her brain from the quiescent stupor of depression. 'I don't know what you're talking about, Marcia,' she declared unsteadily. 'I didn't tell Matt anything that wasn't true.'

'You told him about your father's will—or lack of it!'

'He asked me. He asked me what I was going to do, now that Daddy was dead. What was I supposed to say?'

'Did you tell him about Howard?'

'No!'

'No?'

'No. Why would I?'

Marcia's mouth compressed. 'How should I know? You seem to have made a pretty good job of assassinating my character.'

'Oh, come on, Marcia. What is it? What's happened? What did Matt say?' Joanna's knees shook. 'Wasn't he pleased to see you?'

Marcia did not answer her. She turned her back on her stepdaughter, and walked instead to the vanity unit, betraying her agitation only in the way her hands fidgeted with the brushes and cosmetics she found there.

Joanna drew a steadying breath. Something had gone wrong, that much was obvious, but it was too soon yet for her to feel any exhilaration at the outcome. The fact that Matthew and Marcia had had a row meant very little. It probably had been too unrealistic to imagine that two people could meet again after so many years without finding some disagreement. Nevertheless, she knew a trembling sense of anticipation.

'What happened?' she probed again. 'Wh-where is Matt?' Could he still be downstairs? Her pulses raced. 'Have you had dinner?'

'Don't talk rubbish!' Marcia swung round at last, apparently having recovered some sense of composure. 'Of course we haven't had dinner. We had a drink in the bar, and that only because the foyer was too public a place to conduct the kind of conversation Matt had in mind.'

Joanna inched her way to the bed. 'I—don't understand——'

'Of course you do.' Marcia gazed at her

contemptuously, and Joanna wondered suddenly how much Matthew had told her stepmother. If he had admitted to her about their relationship, why hadn't Marcia already said so, instead of accusing her of talking about her behind her back? 'He was at pains to tell me what he thought of me as a mother,' Marcia continued grimly. 'According to him, you'd run away because I'd made your life so miserable you couldn't take it any more!' Her lips twisted. 'I soon put him straight on that score!'

Joanna caught her breath. 'You didn't——'

'—tell him about you working for Evan? Why not?' She laughed into Joanna's horrified face. 'Don't look like that. I can't help it if Evan doesn't get his story. And you don't have to worry either, thanks to me. I'll pay your expenses, just to get him off our backs. He can do his own dirty work in future.'

Joanna sank down weakly on to the bed. It wasn't as if she hadn't anticipated this, but somehow, in the pain of learning about Matthew's previous involvement with Marcia, it had become obscured. When she sent her stepmother off to meet Matthew, she had not considered what Marcia might do if he rejected her, and her own misery at his betrayal had blinded her to the most obvious outcome. Oh God! she groaned inwardly, what must he think of *her* now? Would she ever be able to convince him that she had not intended to go through with Evan's demands?

'Don't look so stricken!' Marcia was unfeeling. 'It's not my fault if things haven't turned out the way you'd like them to do. You should have thought of that before you started begging for sympathy. Imagine telling Matt that I didn't give a damn about you! I soon told him what an ungrateful little devil you were!'

Joanna drew her legs up to her chin and buried her face on her knees. 'Go away, Marcia,' she said, unable to sustain this conversation any longer. 'You've said what you came to say. Now leave me alone.'

'Aren't you going to ask me if I'm seeing him again?' Marcia countered.

'I really don't care,' muttered Joanna, in a muffled voice. 'Just go away and leave me, please. I—I've got to think what I'm going to do.'

'Well, we made no plans before he left,' said Marcia, almost as if Joanna had asked the question. 'But I can wait. Once he's had time to think about me—about what we once had—well, then he might change his mind.'

'Marcia!'

'All right, I'm going.' Marcia strolled towards the door, her temper expunged by the sight of the girl in such an obvious state of distress. 'As for you, my dear, I suggest you make arrangements to return to England immediately.' She paused. 'Mrs Morris will look after you. I know she'll be delighted to have you back. She's been most disapproving since you went away.'

'Marcia, please——'

'I'm going.' Marcia opened the door. 'I'll see you for breakfast. We'll have it together.' She hesitated. 'Before you leave.'

The sound of the door closing was like a death knell to Joanna's hopes. Blind and deaf to anything but her own misery, she rocked back and forth in an agony of self-reproach, understanding, belatedly, that she really was to blame for everything that had happened. Today; if she had only told Matthew today, Marcia's words would have meant nothing. As it was, her stepmother had broadcast Joanna's deception, destroyed any confidence Matthew had had in her, and severed their relationship in one fateful swoop. It didn't matter that he hadn't told her about Marcia. Perhaps he would have done later. Perhaps, like her, it was something he had put off. Either way, his feelings for her stepmother were not as strong as they had once been. Evidently the ardour of his youth had been tempered by experience, and he was no longer as willing to forgive and forget.

When Joanna finally got off the bed it was nearly ten o'clock —, and her reflection revealed that her eyes were swollen and puffy from her tears. Not exactly a face to launch a thousand ships, she thought bitterly, sliding her spectacles on to her nose. But it was the only one she had, and for what she had in mind, it would have to do.

Misery had given way to a tenuous kind of desperation, and as she rummaged in the closet for her jeans, and pushed her arms into the sleeves of a navy blue sweater, she forced herself not to think beyond the next few hours. In all honesty, what she most wanted to do was crawl into a dark corner until the desolation she was feeling eased a fraction. But time was something she didn't have, and if she wanted to try and salvage something from this sorry affair, hiding away in corners wasn't going to help. She had to see Matthew, even if it was for the last time. She had to try and make him believe her story. If she didn't, she would never know for sure whether she could have convinced him.

There was no sign of Marcia in the foyer and she approached the desk diffidently, wishing she was not so conscious of her swollen face. 'Excuse me,' she said, disturbing the receptionist with reluctance. 'I'd like to use my car. Could you arrange for someone to get it for me, please?'

The girl measured Joanna with her eyes. 'Miss—Holland, isn't it?' she asked, revealing Carlos Almeira had been talking yet again. 'Just a minute, I'll call one of the valets.'

It was a relief to get behind the wheel of the car, to be *doing* something. And at least it was anonymous, and would save her the necessity of asking a cab-driver to wait. She could hardly depend on Matthew to bring her back.

She reached Palmetto Drive without difficulty. It was a simple matter of following Coral Reef Avenue to the turn-off, and then driving down the unlit lane to Matthew's house. There was no one about, so she had no problem in locating Matthew's gate, and she switched off the engine and sat in silence for a few moments before getting out.

Eventually she summoned up enough courage to climb out of the car and ring the bell. She had left the car's headlights on, needing their reassuring illumination to sustain her, and she waited by the padlocked entry, trying to calm her nerves. Her palms were damp, and there was a discomfiting trickle of moisture along her spine, that caused her to shiver even though she was sweating.

She didn't know how long she had been standing there before she rang the bell again. She guessed it must have been about five minutes, but no one had responded to her summons, and she was getting desperate. The shadows cast by the swaying palms created illusions of dark figures all around her, and she tugged the bell despairingly, fighting the urge to escape.

The lights came on as she was about to get into

the car, and her hands trembled as she turned back and gripped the bars of the gate. Someone was coming. Oh, please, let it be Matthew, she begged, peering through the vine-covered trellises that hid most of the path from view, let him be prepared to listen to her!

She heard his breathing before he reached the gate. It was heavy and laboured, as if he had been running, and she drew back uncertainly, wishing she was more prepared. Could she offer any real justification for what she had done? she fretted anxiously. Could she find any comfortable excuse for the job she had undertaken? Would Matthew accept that she had been desperate, that Evan's option had seemed the only alternative? Put into words it sounded so feeble, and after what Marcia had said, would he believe that meeting him had made so irrevocable a difference?

'Matt——' she whispered, as he appeared from between the spiked bushes. 'Oh, Matt, thank heavens it's you!'

But it was not Matt. As the man came nearer, she realised with dismay that it was not Matthew's tawny eyes that looked out at her from beneath thickened lids, it was not Matthew's lean mouth that gathered in the semblance of a frown, or Matthew's hand that was unable to hide its clawlike curvature. With the lights of the house behind him, it was impossible to see him clearly, but the man who halted some yards from the gate bore the scars of his illness like a shield. He cowered behind them, as if afraid of witnessing her contempt, and his voice when he spoke was indistinct and distant.

'Matt's not here,' he said, shrinking back against the foliage. 'I think you'd better go.'

Joanna allowed her breath to escape cautiously. 'Where is he?' she asked, pressing her face against the bars. 'I must see him—I must speak to him. Please, Mr Massey, tell him I'm here. It's very important.'

'You know my name?' The man shifted uneasily.

'Yes, Matt told me,' replied Joanna desperately. 'Please, if you won't let me in, at least ask Matt to come and speak to me,'

'He's not here,' answered the man, glancing behind him. 'He went to the hotel to meet someone. I thought it was you.'

'It was me,' exclaimed Joanna, sighing. 'But I didn't see him. He met someone else—my stepmother. Oh——' she broke off as she realised this would mean nothing to him, '—don't you have any idea where he might be?'

'No.' The man moved his head from side to side. 'I only know he's not here. And if he did not meet you, then perhaps it is all for the best.'

'What do you mean?'

'He was going to tell you he couldn't see you again,' he stated simply, and Joanna gasped. 'Go back to England, Miss Holland. Believe me, you're wasting your time here.'

'No,' Joanna shook her head, 'I can't—I won't. I have to see him—to explain. I respect his work, I respect what he's doing, and I admire him for it. I would never betray his confidence to anyone, never! Oh, I know Marcia's told him that I came to Florida to spy on him for Evan Price, but that was before I met him, before I—I fell in love with him. I need to tell him that, don't you see? I need to beg for his forgiveness——'

'There's nothing to forgive,' declared Massey

flatly. 'I know nothing about why you came to Florida, or what Matt's reactions might be if he suspected you had been lying to him. That is not important. What is important is that your relationship with Matt could only have brought unhappiness and pain, for both of you. Wait——' this as she would have interrupted him, 'Matt has not been honest with you, Miss Holland. He did not leave England because of me, because he wanted to treat me. It would not have been necessary for him to hide himself away if all he wanted to do was research! What did he tell you about me? Did he tell you how I refused to accept the evidence of my own eyes? Did he tell you how I hid the symptoms of my condition for months before admitting the truth? I was a fool, I know that now. But people who contract leprosy are tempted to be foolish. Have you any idea what it's like to be called a leper? Of course you haven't. You've never experienced the humiliation of people turning away from you in the street, of witnessing the revulsion in a healthy person's eyes when they see your pitiful condition! It's a living hell, Miss Holland. And so unfair. Cancer is a terrible disease, but no one turns aside from someone who has cancer. Leprosy, in spite of the fact that it is controllable, arouses all the old superstitious beliefs. It's been around since biblical times, yet it still attracts the kind of persecution that in any other context would be denounced as a violation of human rights!'

Joanna shook her head. 'Oh, please——'

'Please, what, Miss Holland? Am I boring you?'

'No——'

'But you don't see what this has to do with you, do you?'

'Not exactly.'

'Then I'll explain.' He took an unsteady step towards her. 'Miss Holland, what you don't know is that Matt contracted the disease, too.'

'No!'

'Oh, yes.' Massey was trembling with emotion. 'He was infected in Africa, while he was working at a hospital there. And because, like all of us who dread the critical eyes of the world, he couldn't bear the fear or pity of his friends, he ran away. He'd been offered a research fellowship in London, but he gave it up. He bought this house, and for the past three years he's been working here in virtual isolation. That's why I say you're wasting your time here, that's why your friendship with Matt can have no future!'

Joanna hardly knew how she got back to the hotel. It must have been pure instinct that guided her to take the correct turnings, and handing over her keys at the desk, she scarcely noticed the surprised look the receptionist gave her.

'Are you all right, Miss Holland?' she asked anxiously, viewing Joanna's wild eyes and tear-stained cheeks with some concern. 'You didn't have an accident, did you? If there's anything you need, just say the word.'

'I'm okay.' Joanna forced herself to respond with an effort. 'Was there—I mean, have there been any calls for me while I've been out?'

'No, I'm afraid not.' The girl looked apologetic. 'Oh, there was a man here earlier, asking for you. But I guess you saw him.'

Joanna bent her head. 'Oh, yes,' she said unsteadily, 'I know about that.' She moved towards the lifts. 'Goodnight.'

'Goodnight, Miss Holland.'

The girl watched her enter the lift, and Joanna breathed a sigh of relief when the metal doors closed her in on her misery. Oh, Matt, she breathed achingly, why didn't you tell me? Don't you know nothing could make me love you less.

Evan Price rang as Joanna was brushing her hair the next morning. For one heart-stopping moment, she thought it might be Matthew, but a distant crackling on the line was evidence enough that it was not.

'Joanna!' he exclaimed, his husky tone revealing that he had not yet got rid of his cold. 'Where on earth have you been? I tried to get in touch with you twice yesterday.'

'I was out,' said Joanna dully. 'You didn't leave any message.'

'No. I didn't think there was much point,' admitted Evan ruefully. 'I suppose you've seen Marcia. I couldn't stop her, you know. Cynthia told her where you were, and she practically blackmailed me into revealing what you were doing.'

'I know. It's all right.' Joanna didn't have the energy to get into any kind of discussion over Marcia: 'What do you want, Evan? I don't have much time. I'm driving back to Miami today, and I should be back in England by tomorrow or the next day.'

'What!' Evan sounded furious. 'You're not leaving just because that stepmother of yours has turned up? Ignore her. You're there to do a job. Must I remind you again, that's what I'm paying you for!'

'I'm resigning,' replied Joanna flatly. 'I don't

want your job, Evan. I don't like this kind of work. I know that means you won't pay me, but Marcia says she will cover my expenses.'

'The hell she will!'

'It's no good, Evan. Matt—Matthew Wilder knows why I came here now. Marcia told him. Even if I was prepared to go on with the job, which I'm not, I'd be wasting my time.'

Evan swore angrily. 'Why the hell did she do that? Blow your cover, I mean. What's Wilder to her? I didn't know she'd even met the man.'

'Well, she has.' Joanna spoke tightly. 'Apparently she's known him for a number of years.'

'And I suppose she thought she'd be doing him a favour by letting him know what you were doing.'

Joanna shook her head. 'Something like that,' she agreed, unwilling to argue about it. 'Is that all, Evan. I really do have to go.' She paused. 'I— Marcia is waiting for me.'

'Bitch!' muttered Evan vehemently. 'Marcia, I mean. Poking her nose into other people's business. Just when you seemed to be having some success. Tricia—my secretary, that is—Tricia told me you'd rung while I was laid up. Oh, of course, you know that, don't you? That's how all this came out, what with Cynthia speaking to your stepmother about it. You've no idea how angry I was. Anyway, you might as well tell me what it was you had to report. Even if I am going to have to think of some other line on this.'

'I—I——' It was on the tip of Joanna's tongue to tell him she had nothing to report, but something, some inner caution warned her not to antagonise him. How much better it would be if she could give him some information which might throw him off the scent completely, for she had little doubt that word of Matthew's illness was exactly the kind of sensational story Evan had hoped to unearth. How he had latched on to it, she didn't know, unless her father had said something in the diaries to arouse his suspicions. But knowing her father as she had, she doubted he would have put anything incriminating down in writing, so Evan could only be whistling in the dark.

'Well?' He was waiting for her answer now, and Joanna nervously cleared her throat.

'Well, I rang to tell you I'd discovered that Matt—*Uncle* Matt, that is—may be having an affair with the woman I thought was his housekeeper—Mrs Massey.'

'Having an affair?' echoed Evan scornfully, and Joanna hastened on:

'Yes. She's a married woman. I—quite wealthy, I believe. I got the impression that was why he had left England.'

'Joanna, nobody cares about adultery these days.' Evan was impatient. 'Are you seriously asking me to consider that Wilder would care about a thing like that?'

'Maybe—maybe Mrs Massey would.'

'Hmm.' Evan didn't sound too convinced. 'It's possible, I suppose. After you gave me her name earlier, I did make some enquiries, but I didn't come up with anything.'

'Perhaps—perhaps she's financing his research,' suggested Joanna tentatively. 'Perhaps moving to Florida was part of the deal.'

'She's an American?'

'Oh—I'm not sure.' Joanna floundered. 'She could be. I've hardly spoken to her.'

'Hmm.' Evan was evidently considering it. 'What kind of research is he doing?'

'Well, I don't know that he's doing any,' said Joanna hurriedly. 'I'm only trying to offer suggestions.'

'But she's a good-looking woman, you say?'

'I didn't say. But—yes, she is quite—handsome.'

'And young?'

'Younger than him,' agreed Joanna gratefully.

'Well.' Evan seemed to be giving the matter serious thought. 'It could be as you say. I mean, your father was hardly likely to keep Wilder's address in a thing like a diary if the man had anything to hide.'

'Wh-what do you mean?' Joanna spoke faintly, but she had to ask.

'Wilder,' said Evan snorting. 'Oh, there were all sorts of rumours at the time he disappeared. Someone said he'd contracted one of those filthy diseases he used to work with, but if he has this woman living with him . . .' His voice trailed away.

'He has.' Joanna endeavoured to sound only casually interested. 'But what sort of disease do you mean?'

'Leprosy,' replied Evan, without hesitation. 'That was my original idea. But you knocked that on the head when you said you'd had dinner at his house. I mean, he wouldn't have invited you there—and you would have noticed.'

He broke off, and Joanna had to bite her tongue to prevent herself from contradicting his statement. No wonder there was so much confusion about the disease, she thought helplessly, if men like Evan Price were as ignorant as the rest.

'Oh, what the hell!' he said now, interrupting her troubled musings. 'I've a good mind to drop the whole inquiry. Lepers, leprosy; the world can do without them. Okay, Joanna. You come on home. We'll find some other way for you to earn your money.'

'Well—thank you.' Joanna forced herself to sound grateful. 'But it won't be necessary. Marcia—Marcia's decided public opinion is against her. She's offered to pay for me to go to art college, so I shan't need to earn the money, after all.'

'Oh, well, it's done some good, then,' observed Evan drily. 'I suppose she'll be coming home with you.'

'I—probably,' agreed Joanna uncertainly, and breathed a sigh of relief when she could put the receiver down.

CHAPTER ELEVEN

No sooner had Joanna finished with the call than Marcia knocked at the door. Going to open it, she reflected that her stepmother had probably been eavesdropping on her conversation, and Marcia's first words confirmed it.

'That was Evan on the phone, wasn't it?' she demanded, walking into the room. 'I heard the phone ring as I came along the corridor. These walls are paper-thin. I've no doubt your next-door neighbour heard every word.'

'As you did, Marcia?' asked Joanna bitterly, unable to forgive her stepmother for what she had told Matthew. 'What have you been doing? Listening at my door? Weren't you afraid someone might come along and see you?'

'Why should I be afraid?' countered Marcia sharply. 'You are my stepdaughter, Joanna. I have a right to know who you're talking to.'

'You have no rights as far as I'm concerned,' retorted Joanna, dragging her case on to the bed to finish her packing. 'What do you want, Marcia? As you can see, I'm busy. If you expect me to join you for breakfast, you're going to be disappointed.'

'Don't be like that.' Marcia linked and unlinked her fingers, her attitude suggesting that she had something more important to talk about. 'Joanna, what was that you were telling Evan about Matt's housekeeper? Do I take it our elusive friend has got a mistress?'

'You can take it whatever way you like,' declared Joanna, gathering her cosmetics together and bundling them into her vanity case. 'Matthew Wilder's affairs are nothing to do with us, Marcia. Now, will you please get out of my way.'

'Cool it, Joanna. I don't know what you're getting so uptight about. I didn't know this job was so important to you.'

'It wasn't.' Joanna's anger surfaced. 'As a matter of fact I hated it. I hated every minute of it. And if you hadn't been so greedy, I'd never have accepted it in the first place!'

'Dear me!' Marcia grimaced. 'Such high ideals! Are you sure it isn't the fact that you won't be seeing Tom O'Connor again that's getting you so upset?'

'His name's Connolly,' muttered Joanna, between her teeth. 'And Tom was just a—a holiday acquaintance, nothing more.'

'Oh, well.' Marcia seemed to accept this. 'But you've met this woman, I take it?'

'What woman?'

'Matt's housekeeper, of course. Oh, yes, you must have done.' Marcia was impatient. 'What's she like?'

Joanna paused in her packing. 'She's very attractive,' she replied at last, getting a certain amount of satisfaction out of seeing Marcia squirm. 'They seemed very—close.'

Marcia snorted. 'I should have guessed as much,' she declared irritably. 'Last night Matt was so cold, so aloof! It wasn't like him at all. I ought to have realised there was someone else. And it's like him to take pity on some lame duck. I suppose it's nothing serious.'

'What's not serious?'

Joanna was barely listening to her. Her heart was pounding so loudly at the news that Matthew had not responded to her stepmother's invitation, she was deaf to anything else.

'Whatever's wrong with her, of course,' exclaimed Marcia impatiently. 'I heard what you said about her being ill, Joanna. I imagine, as Matt is a doctor, she must be a patient. How unethical!'

'Oh!'

Joanna's lips formed a perfect circle. Now she understood. Having seen Matthew for herself, Marcia had no doubts about his fitness. Instead, when she had heard Joanna mention the word 'disease', she had assumed they must be discussing Mrs Massey's illness. Thank heavens for Elena! thought Joanna fervently. Marcia could have been just as destructive in her own way as Evan Price.

'Well?'

Marcia was waiting for an answer, and Joanna quickly improvised. 'Evan has only heard gossip,' she declared. 'He—he said something about a nervous complaint. But Mrs Massey looked well enough to me.'

'Did she?' Marcia grimaced. 'Oh, well, why should I care if he chooses to waste his life following lost causes? In my opinion, he always wasted his talent, working in those underdeveloped countries. Do you know, he could have had a practice in Harley Street? He was offered the chance. But no,' she uttered a sound of aggravation, 'he had no interest in making his fortune. Is it any wonder I chose your father?'

Joanna's hands stilled. 'Was that why?'

'I've admitted as much.' Marcia shrugged. 'Andrew was much more civilised. He didn't expect me to go and live with him in some remote outpost, to live with people who hadn't even enough water to drink, let alone to wash with. I wanted to travel, yes; but in style and comfort. Not in the back of a jeep, across miles of scrubby desert!'

'So you turned him down?'

Marcia walked towards the door. 'I suppose, if I was absolutely honest, I'd admit we turned one another down.' She made a moue with her lips. 'Of course, I'd never admit this to anyone else, but as I'm never likely to see him again, what does it matter?'

Joanna caught her breath. 'But you said——'

'I know, I know. But no woman likes to admit she's been jilted. And if I'd been willing to go with him, I probably shouldn't have been.'

'And my father?'

'Oh, Andrew made a pretty good job of picking up the pieces. He was pretty mad at Matt for a while, but that passed, as you know.'

'So it was my father who stopped inviting Matt—Matthew to the house.' said Joanna carefully.

Marcia grimaced. 'He was jealous. He wouldn't risk bringing us together again. I had—exaggerated the story to him, too. He was very sympathetic.'

'I see.'

It was much clearer now. Matthew's distrust of Marcia; the reasons why he had never mentioned their relationship to her; her father's infatuation for the woman he believed had been wronged; it was all beginning to fall into place, and Joanna didn't like the picture it was making.

'I'll leave you to finish your packing,' said Marcia now, opening the door. 'You will let me know when you're leaving, won't you? I may just decide to come with you.'

After she had gone, however, Joanna sank down weakly on to the side of the bed. For some minutes she just sat there gazing blankly into space, while the chaotic jumble of impressions settled into a pattern. If only she had not been so willing to believe Marcia last night; if only she had gone with her anyway, and given Matthew the chance to explain. By cowering up in her room, she had given Marcia free licence to say and do anything to justify her non-appearance, and how did she really know what Marcia had said?

Getting up from the bed, she walked out on to the balcony and leaned unhappily on the rail. Already the sun-deck below her was busy with holidaymakers, all spreading out their towels and themselves, to get a better tan. Children splashed about in the pool; someone was playing a transistor; and down on the beach a group of joggers were making their way along the shoreline. It was such a peaceful scene, the perfect backdrop for the perfect holiday. If only she was as carefree as those holidaymakers, she thought. If only she and Matthew could start again . . .

Unable to bear the torture of her thoughts, Joanna picked up her bag and left her room. Going down in the lift, she realised Marcia would probably be having breakfast in the restaurant, but the coffee shop was anonymous, and a hot drink might revive her flagging spirits.

After ordering herself some coffee, she found a table in the corner and sat down. Happily the little snack bar was practically empty, and after the waitress had brought her coffee Joanna was able to linger over it, without feeling anyone's eyes upon her.

'Miss Holland?'

The familiar summons caused Joanna to lift her head resignedly, and she watched Carlos Almeira crossing the room towards her with weary acquiescence. Surely he hadn't anticipated the fact that she was leaving? she thought. She had yet to tell the management she was changing her mind yet again.

'Good morning, Miss Holland,' Carlos greeted her smilingly, his unfailing good humour grating on her nerves. 'I have been looking for you,' he added, reaching her table. 'You have a visitor.'

Joanna's heart leapt and then subsided. 'A—a visitor?' she echoed, refusing to believe what her senses were telling her was true. 'Who—who is it?'

'Me,' declared a voice behind Carlos, and looking up she saw Matthew waiting for her to notice him. He looked pale and haggard, his bloodshot eyes evidence of the restless night he had spent, but his identity was unmistakable, and her heart palpitated wildly.

'Matt!' she breathed, and observing her expectant face, Carlos gave a characteristic grimace.

'I think you know,' he remarked, extricating himself from his role as mediator. 'Excuse me, please. I must return to my duties.'

'Matt,' whispered Joanna again, as Carlos made himself scarce, and with an inclination of his head Matthew moved to pull out a chair and straddle it.

'The same,' he agreed, his expression far from encouraging. 'I gather you're feeling better this morning, although I must say you don't look it.'

'Thanks.' Joanna picked up her spoon and began to stir her coffee to give herself something to do. 'I—I'm sorry I couldn't join you last night. But—but I thought you would prefer it!'

'Like hell you did!' swore Matthew angrily, leaning towards her, and then, when she drew back in alarm, he controlled himself again. 'Just tell me how you found out, Joanna. That's all I want to know. Just tell me, and then I'll leave you in peace!'

Joanna gulped. 'Found out? Found out what?'

'That I had had leprosy, of course,' snapped Matthew, in a low savage tone. 'Yesterday— yesterday I came close to believing that, in spite of everything, I might have a chance of a normal existence.' He shook his head. 'You destroyed that. You destroyed everything that was decent and good in my life. I could have killed you! If I'd have got my hands on you last night, I'd have wrung your selfish little neck!'

Joanna stared at him. 'Matt, I don't know what you're talking about——'

'Of course you do,' he stated bleakly. 'Why else did you send your stepmother down to make your excuses? What happened? Did Elena phone you? Did what she told you make you feel so ill you couldn't face me?'

'No!' Joanna was horrified. 'Marcia didn't tell you that!'

'She didn't need to. It was obvious, wasn't it? What other reason could there be for you to walk out on me? After—well, after what had happened between us, there has to be no other explanation. And if you're going to tell me now you've changed your mind, forget it! I can't turn my feelings on and off like a tap!'

'Matt!' Joanna pushed her coffee cup aside and got to her feet. 'You must know why I asked Marcia to meet you. She told me about your affair——'

'What affair?' Matthew looked up at her between drawn brows. 'Joanna, if this——'

'It's what she told me,' insisted Joanna unsteadily. 'She—she said that you and she used to be engaged——'

'Engaged!' Matthew said an ugly word Joanna had never heard before. 'We were never *engaged*! What lies has she been telling now? Our relationship lasted a few months, that's all. Just long enough for her to realise I wasn't about to abandon my research to take up some highly-paid job in the City, and for me to discover what a money-grabbing little bitch she was!'

'But you introduced her to Daddy.'

'Sure, I did that,' Matthew nodded grimly. 'And lived to regret it.'

'Because—because you realised——'

'Because it was almost the cause of a rift between your father and me,' snapped Matthew forcefully. 'I tried to make him see what she was like, but Drew wouldn't listen. Marcia had managed to convince him that I was really jealous!' He shook his head in grim reminiscence. 'If he'd only known!'

Joanna gripped her bag tightly. 'But don't you see? If she could convince my father, why couldn't she have convinced me, too? She—she let me think you were—were crazy about her. That once you realised she was free and available——'

'But she doesn't know about us!' exclaimed Matthew, swinging his leg off the chair and standing up. 'Does she?'

'No! No!' Joanna pushed agitated fingers into her hair. 'That was why I couldn't say anything, don't you see? I—I let her think I'd been out with Tom all day.'

'Connolly?' Matthew's eyes darkened. 'So that's where she got the name from!'

'What name?'

'Connolly's name, of course.' Matthew sighed heavily. 'Joanna, we've both been the victims of misconception. Marcia convinced me that you'd talked about nothing else but this young American you'd met at the hotel.'

'And that's what you got so angry about?'

'Yes. No. Oh, you know what I thought.' Matthew lifted his hand to massage the muscles at the back of his neck, and his action drew Joanna's attention to the little white scar near his elbow. She had seen it before, the day she met him on the bench below his house. But now, with her new knowledge, her eyes were drawn compulsively towards it.

Matthew, intercepting her stare, dropped his arm abruptly, his mouth compressing in a thin line. 'So now you know,' he muttered, taking a step back from her. 'I've had leprosy, too. That mark you can see was caused by the flame from a gas-burner. I didn't feel it until it was too late, and by then my arm was burned. It's the only visible scar that I have.'

'Oh, Matt——' Joanna stepped towards him to put her hand on his arm, but he evaded her.

'Don't touch me,' he said. 'I don't need your pity. Save it for the poor souls who don't recover There are plenty of them, heaven knows!'

'Matt, it doesn't matter——'

'What doesn't matter?'

'Your having leprosy.' Joanna pressed her hands together. 'Honestly, you've got to believe me. It doesn't make any difference.'

'Not now, you mean?'

'Not ever,' exclaimed Joanna fiercely. 'I didn't even know you'd been infected until I spoke to Mr Massey.'

Matthew frowned. 'Don't you mean—*Mrs* Massey?'

'No. I know what I mean. Didn't he tell you? I came to your house last night.'

Matthew's brows descended. 'You came to *my house* last night!'

'Yes. Didn't you know? But I thought—oh, well, I did. After—after you'd left the hotel, Marcia came to see me. She—she told me she'd told you about—about Evan—about why I came out to Florida. I knew I had to see you then, to try and explain about my reasons for accepting the job, to assure you that I had no intention of going on with it, but you weren't there. That man—Henri Massey—he came to speak to me. It was he who told me about you—about the leprosy and everything.'

'Henri?' Matthew shook his head disbelievingly. 'But why would he do that?'

Joanna sighed. 'I think he was trying to protect you. I think he thought that if I ever found out the truth, I'd want to leave you. He didn't want you to be hurt. He knew you hadn't told me——'

'How could I?' Matthew was savage.

'—and he was trying to help. I didn't know what to think. I just told him to tell you I loved you, and then I came back here. I waited. I waited for hours. But when you didn't call, I thought—I assumed——'

'Wait a minute!' Matthew passed a bewildered hand over his eyes. 'You're saying that you had some reason for coming out here?'

'Yes.'

'That—someone sent you out here to find me? Because they knew I was a friend of your father's?'

'Evan Price. He promised to pay my expenses at art school, if I'd come out here and find out what you were doing. I was desperate. I——' Joanna broke off suddenly. 'Marcia didn't tell you?'

'Marcia told me nothing,' said Matthew flatly. 'She was too busy trying to convince me she'd turned over a new leaf.'

'Oh!' Joanna turned away now, tears of pain and frustration filling her eyes. Once again, it seemed, Marcia had succeeded in destroying a relationship, and now she had blurted out the words that would condemn her for ever.

'Joanna!' With an exclamation of impatience Matthew swung her round to face him, and when he saw the tears staining her cheeks, he uttered an unholy oath. 'Come on,' he said. 'Let's get out of here. We have to talk, and I have no intention of letting what I have to say create a diversion for your fellow guests!'

Joanna gazed up at him anxiously. 'We could go up to my room,' she ventured.

'You want that?' Matthew was grave.

'Oh, yes. *Yes!*' she breathed, sliding her hand into his and with a nod of acquiescence Matthew drew her after him towards the exit.

The foyer was not busy at this hour of the morning, and if Carlos thought there was anything suspicious about Joanna taking a strange man up to her room, he was tactful enough not to voice it. Instead they gained the safety of the lift without mishap, and within the privacy of its metal walls, Matthew pulled Joanna into his arms.

'Don't stop me,' he groaned, parting her lips with eager insistence, and in the searching intimacy of his kiss, Joanna had no room to think of retribution.

His mouth was still possessing hers when the lift stopped at the fourth floor. The doors slid open to reveal Joanna's slim frame moulded to the muscular hardness of Matthew's thighs, her arms around his waist, his lean brown hand spread familiarly against her bare back beneath the hem of her thin cotton shirt. His other hand was behind her head, tangled in the silken darkness of her hair, holding her face up to his with mindless, passionate abandon.

'Joanna! *Matt!*'

Marcia's voice cracked on his name, and she fell back disbelievingly as the two in the lift were brought abruptly to their senses. Joanna, shocked out of the drugged ecstasy that Matthew's kisses had evoked, swayed a little unsteadily as she stepped into the corridor, but Matthew's arm across her shoulders was reassuring and possessive.

'Hello, Marcia,' said Matthew coolly, instantly aware of the woman's hostility. 'Don't look so shocked. I'm afraid Joanna forgot to tell you we're very close friends.'

A muscle was working in Marcia's cheek, and looking at her stepmother, Joanna could almost feel her antagonism. Casting a swift look at Matthew, she saw that he was aware of it, too, but unlike Joanna, he seemed unmoved by Marcia's tight-lipped animosity.

'You bastard!' Marcia got out at last, and then turned her fury on Joanna. 'And as for you——'

'I don't think there's anything to be gained by losing your temper, Marcia,' Matthew interrupted her with deceptive mildness. 'Don't pretend you care about Joanna. You probably care as much about her as you did about her father.'

'You keep out of this, Matthew——'

'I think not.'

'Joanna depends on me.'

'Not any longer.'

'What do you mean?'

Both women turned to look at him then, and Matthew held Joanna's eyes as he said: 'I'm hoping to marry her, if she'll have me. I haven't asked her yet, but I will.'

'Oh, Matt!'

Joanna's eyes shone with happiness, but Marcia had not yet finished. 'You're crazy!' she declared. 'She's far too young for you! You must be out of your mind!'

'Perhaps I am,' said Matthew levelly. 'Perhaps she won't have me. But at least I'm going to try.'

'She hasn't a penny, you know.'

'I know.'

'You're mad!' Marcia drew a furious breath. 'I don't suppose she's told you she came out here to spy on you for a magazine, has she?'

'As a matter of fact, she has,' replied Matthew flatteningly, feeling Joanna trembling in his grasp. 'Perhaps if you'd offered to help her, she wouldn't have had to take the assignment. But, unlikely as it may seem to you, I'm glad she did. Otherwise we might never have met again.'

Joanna's lips parted. 'Do you mean that?' she breathed, not realising she was ignoring Marcia, and Matthew bent to bestow a lingering kiss at the corner of her mouth.

'Can you think of any other way?' he asked, and Marcia made an angry sound of disgust.

'Get out of my way!' she exclaimed, stepped

forward to ring for the lift that had gone away again while they were talking. 'I can't stand to listen to any more of this! I just wonder what Mrs Massey will say when you bring another woman into the house.'

'Mrs Massey?' Matthew arched his brows, and Joanna shook her head.

'I'll explain later,' she murmured, and he nodded.

'We won't be living with Mrs Massey, or her husband,' he declared, causing Marcia's mouth to open. 'They'll be staying in Florida. Joanna and I are going back to London.'

In her room, with the door secured against any unwanted intrusion, Joanna turned to stare at him with wide eyes. 'Going back to London?' she echoed faintly. 'Oh, Matt, is that really what you want to do?'

'Is it what you want to do?' he asked, holding her loosely with his hands at her waist, and she made a helpless gesture.

'I'll do whatever you want, live wherever you want to live,' she declared simply. 'I love you— you know I do. I just can't believe that you've forgiven me.'

'Forgiven you? For agreeing to spy on me?' Matthew grimaced. 'I meant what I said, you know. Without that, we might never have seen one another again.'

'I know, but——'

'I guess it's about time I came out of hiding,' said Matthew heavily. 'But first of all, are you sure about this? After what Henri must have told you, haven't you any second thoughts?'

'None,' said Joanna, moving closer to him. 'Oh, Matt! I thought I'd lost you. I wanted to die. Don't ever make me go through that again!'

'Make you go through it?' Matthew cupped her face in his palms and lowered his mouth to hers. 'My darling, where do you think I've been since last night? Driving myself to exhaustion behind the wheel of the car, staying away from the house because I didn't want to see Elena's smug face!'

'Elena!' Joanna understood. 'You thought she'd rung me.'

'I couldn't think of anything else. Even now, I'm not convinced she wasn't behind Henri's revelations.' He sighed. 'You might as well know, once—only once—I made a fool of myself with Elena. I was drunk. I know that's no excuse, but it was just after we got here, just after I'd given up everything I'd ever worked for. I guess I was looking for oblivion. I didn't find it. You can't run away from life. But Elena—well, when she learned about you——'

'—she was jealous,' Joanna finished, pressing her face against the opened neck of his shirt. She touched her lips to his skin. 'You don't have to tell me this, you know.'

'I want to,' he muttered huskily. 'I want there to be no secrets between us. I want you to know what kind of a milksop you're getting.' He shook his head. 'I thought I was so strong. I thought, if it happened to me, I'd be able to handle it. But I couldn't. When it happened, I was just like everyone else—I went to pieces.'

Joanna slid her arms around him. 'I wish I'd been there.'

'I don't. I wasn't fit to live with in those days. I was like a mole, burrowing into the ground, cutting myself off from anyone who might—who just might—suspect what had happened.'

'Matt, it's understandable——'

'But indefensible,' he inserted flatly. 'I've hidden away long enough. It's time I faced reality. It's time I found out who my friends really are.'

'Are you sure?'

'Yes, I'm sure.' His lips twisted. 'I'm cured, if anyone will believe it. A cure is possible. I'm lucky, I know that. In a case like Henri's, there is no cure, only the chance to arrest the disease's progress. But if it'd been diagnosed sooner, if he hadn't been so damned scared of public reaction——'

'Was he working with you then?'

'No.' Matthew frowned. 'He was a patient, in the hospital in Malawi where I'd been working. I was back in London when—when I found out about myself. I thought of Henri at once. I knew he would jump at the chance of being able to work again. Elena came with him, and with the help of a South American friend, I set up my own laboratory here, and began my own programme of research.'

Joanna tilted her head to look up at him. 'And have you made any progress?'

'Progress is very slow,' admitted Matthew honestly. 'We haven't yet found a really satisfactory way to culture the bacillus under artificial conditions so that a vaccine can be produced. It may be years before we succeed. Until then, the only answer is to find a swifter way of diagnosing the condition. That's what I've been trying to do.'

Joanna slid her arms around his neck. 'I love you.'

'And I love you,' he breathed. 'But I still don't know if I have the right——'

'What about my rights?' demanded Joanna, her fingers tangled in the hair at the nape of his neck. 'You're all I want, all I've ever wanted.'

Matthew shook his head. 'If we go to London, you must promise me one thing.'

'What?' Joanna spoke absently, her lips bestowing little kisses along the line of his jaw, and Matthew had to concentrate hard to prevent himself from responding to that sensuous invitation.

'You must promise me—you'll go to art school,' he said huskily. 'I mustn't deny you the chance to do what you want to do, just because we're together.'

Joanna drew back to look at him. 'All right. But only because you want me to do it. Compared to my feelings for you, my desire to attend art classes seems totally unimportant.'

'Oh, Joanna . . .'

His mouth found hers with increasing urgency, bearing her back on to the bed behind them so that he could cover her body with his own.

'Heaven help me, I can't let you go,' he muttered, burying his face in the scented hollow between her breasts, and Joanna's smile of contentment was hidden against his lips.

Harlequin® Plus

THE LAND OF WATER

In the days when Spanish galleons roamed the waters of the New World in search of treasure, sailors took great care to avoid the treacherous shoals off the Florida Keys. Many an ill-fated ship foundered and was lost, entrusting its treasure to the ocean's keeping.

The Keys, a chain of small islands, stretch like a delicate necklace from the Florida coast just south of Miami southwestward into the Gulf of Mexico. Those who live there call their home "a land that's mostly water and an earth that's mostly sky."

And indeed, the Overseas Highway linking the Florida Keys crosses forty-three bodies of water from one end of the Keys to the other. One bridge is seven miles long!

Today a traveler who begins at Key Largo in the north will need only a few hours to drive to Key West, which is the southernmost tip of the United States. Along the way is the unusual Pennecamp Coral Reef State Park. There, glass-bottomed boats allow visitors to see the underwater world of a living coral reef.

At the end of the Florida Keys is the famous town of Key West, long a haven for writers and artists. Travelers must be sure to arrive by sundown, when many inhabitants of this spirited and carefree town gather on the western shore to watch the sun dip below the ocean and leave behind a golden-and-lavender sky. On those evenings when the setting sun has created a particularly beautiful spectacle, everyone rises and applauds its "performance." Obviously those Spanish sailors in days of yore didn't know what they were missing!

Take these
4 best-selling novels
FREE

Yes! Four sophisticated, contemporary love stories by four world-famous authors of romance FREE, as your introduction to the Harlequin Presents subscription plan. Thrill to **Anne Mather**'s passionate story BORN OUT OF LOVE, set in the Caribbean....Travel to darkest Africa in **Violet Winspear**'s TIME OF THE TEMPTRESS....Let **Charlotte Lamb** take you to the fascinating world of London's Fleet Street in MAN'S WORLD....Discover beautiful Greece in **Sally Wentworth**'s moving romance SAY HELLO TO YESTERDAY

Harlequin Presents...

The very finest in romance fiction

Join the millions of avid Harlequin readers all over the world who delight in the magic of a really exciting novel. EIGHT great NEW titles published EACH MONTH! Each month you will get to know exciting, interesting, true-to-life people . . . . You'll be swept to distant lands you've dreamed of visiting . . . . Intrigue, adventure, romance, and the destiny of many lives will thrill you through each Harlequin Presents novel.

Get all the latest books before they're sold out!
As a Harlequin subscriber you actually receive your personal copies of the latest Presents novels immediately after they come off the press, so you're sure of getting all 8 each month.

Cancel your subscription whenever you wish!
You don't have to buy any minimum number of books. Whenever you decide to stop your subscription just let us know and we'll cancel all further shipments.

Your FREE gift includes

Anne Mather—Born out of Love
Violet Winspear—Time of the Temptress
Charlotte Lamb—Man's World
Sally Wentworth—Say Hello to Yesterday

FREE Gift Certificate
and subscription reservation

Mail this coupon today!

Harlequin Reader Service

In the U.S.A.
1440 South Priest Drive
Tempe, AZ 85281

In Canada
649 Ontario Street
Stratford, Ontario N5A 6W2

Please send me my 4 Harlequin Presents books free. Also, reserve a subscription to the 8 new Harlequin Presents novels published each month. Each month I will receive 8 new Presents novels at the low price of $1.75 each [*Total— $14.00 a month*]. There are no shipping and handling or any other hidden charges. I am free to cancel at any time, but even if I do, these first 4 books are still mine to keep absolutely FREE without any obligation. **SB610**

NAME _____ (PLEASE PRINT)

ADDRESS _____ APT. NO. _____

CITY _____

STATE/PROV. _____ ZIP/POSTAL CODE _____

Offer expires January 31, 1984

If price changes are necessary you will be notified.